Classic Christmas Tales

-

*An Anthology of Christmas Stories by
Great Authors Including Hans Christian
Andersen, Leo Tolstoy, L. Frank Baum,
Fyodor Dostoyevsky, and O. Henry*

GW00580072

British Library Cataloguing-in-Publication Data
A catalogue record for this book is available from the
British Library

Christmas Tales

Christmas (literally meaning the 'Feast day of Christ') is a Christian holiday that honours the birth of Jesus, celebrated on 25th December. It has become one of the largest festivals in the world, and has an incredibly long and fascinating history – mixing Christianity, paganism, folklore and popular culture. Consequently, the day has amassed a substantial amount of religious and folkloric story telling around the event. Traditions are different from country to country, but they nearly always include feasts, the giving of gifts and church or public festivities such as carols and songs, and storytelling has become a great part of these traditions. Whilst the original tale of the nativity is found in the Gospel of Matthew, namely Matthew 1:18, and the Gospel of Luke, specifically Luke 1:26 and 2:40 (this latter gospel recounts the most of Jesus' birth), there exists a wide range of secular, or non-theological stories, told in popular music, art and books. They are often used to allegorise the biblical Christian mythology of Christmas, but not necessarily - and continue to evolve into the present day. Such stories are frequently classified as mythopoeia (invented mythology), or Christian allegories.

In the early nineteenth century, where this collection commences, the old folklore tradition of storytelling (written and oral) witnessed a massive revival, thanks to the efforts of the Brothers Grimm; two German academics, Jacob (1785–1863) and Wilhelm Grimm (1786–1859), who collected their nations fairy-tales, publishing them in 1812, in *Kinder- und Hausmärche* (Children's and Household Tales). These two men have provided endless inspiration for adults and children alike, but most notably for the current discussion of Christmas Tales, to the Danish Author, Hans Christian Anderson. *Little Match Girl* (first published in 1845) is one of his best known stories; a heavily moralistic, yet beautiful narrative. This work tells the sad, yet ultimately uplifting Christian story of a young and poor girl, who sees a vision of her grandmother in the glow of a single match. The events actually take place on New Years Eve but the story has been widely utilised as a Christmas narrative, and has become embedded into the collective conscious of most Western readers.

The tale introduces a common theme, which the reader will notice in most of the Christmas tales reproduced in this collection; a moralistic or specifically Christian accusation that the meaning of Christmas has been misunderstood. The inspiration for Hans Christian Anderson's story is widely said to have come from *The Star Money,* previously recorded by the Brothers Grimm, about another impoverished young girl who selflessly gives away everything she has to the needy, until she is left with nothing but her love for God. The message of many of these tales directly contradicts a perceived ethos of materialism and personal gratification, common then, as now, in popular depictions of the Christmas holiday.

Dostoyevsky's tale, *The Heavenly Christmas Tree* (1876) and O'Henry's *The Gift of the Maji* (1905) follow a similar narrative structure, emphasising the true Christian values of love and kindness to the Christmas celebration. This, of course, is only one reading of these highly sophisticated stories, and a reason for their continued popularity in the present day is the multiplicty of meanings, both moralising and edifying that one can take from such tales. O'Henry in particular demonstrates to the reader, the important existence and intrinsic worth of his young couple's love for each other.

The Brother's Grimm also embelished the tales they collected, and this is done most poetically in *The Elves and the Shoemaker* (1812). Here, an impoverished yet industrious couple are aided in their endeavours by magical elves who visit them at night. This state can not last forever though, and eventually, due to human involvement, the elves are forced to disappear. Characters such as elves, reindeer and the rotund, jovial character that is *Santa Claus*, really emerged into the popular imagination with the turn of the twentieth century. The trope first appeared in the United States and Canada with Clement Clarke Moore's 1823 poem *A Visit from St Nicholas*, aided by the caricaturist and political caricaturist Thomas Nast, but has since become popularised by such songs as *Santa Claus is Coming to Town* (which first appeared in 1934). The normative aspect of his practice; making lists of naughty or nice children is evidenced in L. Frank Baum's *A Kidnapped Santa Claus* (1904). By this point, much of Santa Clays's mythos was not set in stone, leaving Baum to give his hero a wide variety of immortal support; a home in the Laughing Valley of *Hohaho*, and *ten* reindeer; who could not fly, but leapt in enormous, flight like bounds.

Whilst stories and depictions of Christmas, father christmas, Christianity itself, and the entirety of our festive season have changed, almost without recognition from some of these early depictions - similar themes remain. Ultimately, it remains a holiday celebrating cultural values of the family, kindness and charity, and it is hoped that the reader will gain a certain sense of joy and reflection, but most certainly a good amount festive cheer from these tales. Enjoy.

Contents

The Little Match Girl

By

Hans Christian Andersen

Most terribly cold it was; it snowed, and was nearly quite dark, and evening-- the last evening of the year. In this cold and darkness there went along the street a poor little girl, bareheaded, and with naked feet. When she left home she had slippers on, it is true; but what was the good of that? They were very large slippers, which her mother had hitherto worn; so large were they; and the poor little thing lost them as she scuffled away across the street, because of two carriages that rolled by dreadfully fast.

One slipper was nowhere to be found; the other had been laid hold of by an urchin, and off he ran with it; he thought it would do capitally for a cradle when he some day or other should have children himself. So the little maiden walked on with her tiny naked feet, that were quite red and blue from cold. She carried a quantity of matches in an old apron, and she held a bundle of them in her hand. Nobody had bought anything of her the whole livelong day; no one had given her a single farthing.

She crept along trembling with cold and hunger--a very picture of sorrow, the poor little thing!

The flakes of snow covered her long fair hair, which fell in beautiful curls around her neck; but of that, of course, she never once now thought. From all the windows the candles were gleaming, and it smelt so deliciously of roast goose, for you know it was New Year's Eve; yes, of that she thought.

In a corner formed by two houses, of which one advanced more than the other, she seated herself down and cowered together. Her little feet she had drawn close up to her, but she grew colder and colder, and to go home she did not venture, for she had not sold any matches and could not bring a farthing of money: from her father she would certainly get blows, and at home it was cold too, for above her she had only the roof, through which the wind whistled, even though the largest cracks were stopped up with straw and rags.

Her little hands were almost numbed with cold. Oh! a match might afford her a world of comfort, if she only dared take a single one out of the bundle, draw it against the wall, and warm her fingers by it. She drew one out. "Rischt!" how it blazed, how it burnt! It was a warm, bright flame, like a candle, as she held her hands over it: it was a wonderful light. It seemed really to the little maiden as though she were sitting before a large iron stove, with burnished brass feet and a brass ornament at top. The fire burned with such blessed influence; it warmed so delightfully. The little girl had already stretched out her feet to warm them too; but--the small flame went out, the stove vanished: she had only the remains of the burnt-out match in her hand.

She rubbed another against the wall: it burned brightly, and where the light fell on the wall, there the wall became transparent like a veil, so that she could see into the room. On the table was spread a snow-white tablecloth; upon it was a splendid porcelain service, and the roast goose was steaming famously with its stuffing of apple and dried plums. And what was still more capital to behold was, the goose hopped down from the dish, reeled about on the floor with knife and fork in its breast, till it came up to the poor little girl; when--the match went out and nothing but the thick, cold, damp wall was left behind. She lighted another match. Now there she was sitting under the most magnificent Christmas tree: it was still larger, and more decorated than the one which she had seen through the glass door in the rich merchant's house.

Thousands of lights were burning on the green branches, and gaily-colored pictures, such as she had seen in the shop-windows, looked down upon her. The little maiden stretched out her hands towards them when--the match went out. The lights of the Christmas tree rose higher and higher, she saw them now as stars in heaven; one fell down and formed a long trail of fire.

"Someone is just dead!" said the little girl; for her old grandmother, the only person who had loved her, and who was now no more, had told her, that when a star falls, a soul ascends to God.

She drew another match against the wall: it was again light, and in the lustre there stood the old grandmother, so bright and radiant, so mild, and with such an expression of love.

"Grandmother!" cried the little one. "Oh, take me with you! You go away when the match burns out; you vanish like the warm stove, like the delicious roast goose, and like the magnificent Christmas tree!" And she rubbed the whole bundle of matches quickly against the wall, for she wanted to be quite sure of keeping her grandmother near her. And the matches gave such a brilliant light that it was brighter than at noon-day: never formerly had the grandmother been so beautiful and so tall. She took the little maiden, on her arm, and both flew in brightness and in joy so high, so very high, and then above was neither cold, nor hunger, nor anxiety--they were with God.

But in the corner, at the cold hour of dawn, sat the poor girl, with rosy cheeks and with a smiling mouth, leaning against the wall--frozen to death on the last evening of the old year. Stiff and stark sat the child there with her matches, of which one bundle had been burnt. "She wanted to warm herself," people said. No one had the slightest suspicion of what beautiful things she had seen; no one even dreamed of the splendor in which, with her grandmother she had entered on the joys of a new year.

The Gift of the Magi

By

O. Henry

One dollar and eighty-seven cents. That was all. And sixty cents of it was in pennies. Pennies saved one and two at a time by bulldozing the grocer and the vegetable man and the butcher until one's cheeks burned with the silent imputation of parsimony that such close dealing implied. Three times Della counted it. One dollar and eighty- seven cents. And the next day would be Christmas.

There was clearly nothing to do but flop down on the shabby little couch and howl. So Della did it. Which instigates the moral reflection that life is made up of sobs, sniffles, and smiles, with sniffles predominating.

While the mistress of the home is gradually subsiding from the first stage to the second, take a look at the home. A furnished flat at $8 per week. It did not exactly beggar description, but it certainly had that word on the lookout for the mendicancy squad.

In the vestibule below was a letter-box into which no letter would go, and an electric button from which no mortal finger could coax a ring. Also appertaining thereunto was a card bearing the name "Mr. James Dillingham Young."

The "Dillingham" had been flung to the breeze during a former period of prosperity when its possessor was being paid $30 per week. Now, when the income was shrunk to $20, though, they were thinking seriously of contracting to a modest and unassuming D. But whenever Mr. James Dillingham Young came home and reached his flat above he was called "Jim" and greatly hugged by Mrs. James Dillingham Young, already introduced to you as Della. Which is all very good.

Della finished her cry and attended to her cheeks with the powder rag. She stood by the window and looked out dully at a gray cat walking a gray fence in a gray backyard. Tomorrow would be Christmas Day, and she had only $1.87 with which to buy Jim a present. She had been saving every penny she could for months, with this result. Twenty dollars a week doesn't go far. Expenses had been greater than she had calculated. They always are. Only $1.87 to buy a present for Jim. Her Jim. Many a happy hour she had spent planning for something nice for him. Something fine and rare and sterling-- something just a little bit near to being worthy of the honor of being owned by Jim.

There was a pier-glass between the windows of the room. Perhaps you have seen a pier-glass in an $8 flat. A very thin and very agile person may, by observing his reflection in a rapid sequence of longitudinal strips, obtain a fairly accurate conception of his looks. Della, being slender, had mastered the art.

Suddenly she whirled from the window and stood before the glass. her eyes were shining brilliantly, but her face had lost its color within twenty seconds. Rapidly she pulled down her hair and let it fall to its full length.

Now, there were two possessions of the James Dillingham Youngs in which they both took a mighty pride. One was Jim's gold watch that had been his father's and his grandfather's. The other was Della's hair. Had the queen of Sheba lived in the flat across the airshaft, Della would have let her hair hang out the window some day to dry just to depreciate Her Majesty's jewels and gifts. Had King Solomon been the janitor, with all his treasures piled up in the basement, Jim would have pulled out his watch every time he passed, just to see him pluck at his beard from envy.

So now Della's beautiful hair fell about her rippling and shining like a cascade of brown waters. It reached below her knee and made itself almost a garment for her. And then she did it up again nervously and quickly. Once she faltered for a minute and stood still while a tear or two splashed on the worn red carpet.

On went her old brown jacket; on went her old brown hat. With a whirl of skirts and with the brilliant sparkle still in her eyes, she fluttered out the door and down the stairs to the street.

Where she stopped the sign read: "Mne. Sofronie. Hair Goods of All Kinds." One flight up Della ran, and collected herself, panting. Madame, large, too white, chilly, hardly looked the "Sofronie."

"Will you buy my hair?" asked Della.

"I buy hair," said Madame. "Take yer hat off and let's have a sight at the looks of it."

Down rippled the brown cascade.

"Twenty dollars," said Madame, lifting the mass with a practised hand.

"Give it to me quick," said Della.

Oh, and the next two hours tripped by on rosy wings. Forget the hashed metaphor. She was ransacking the stores for Jim's present.

She found it at last. It surely had been made for Jim and no one else. There was no other like it in any of the stores, and she had turned all of them inside out. It was a platinum fob chain simple and chaste in design, properly proclaiming its value by substance alone and not by meretricious ornamentation--as all good things should do. It was even worthy of The Watch. As soon as she saw it she knew that it must be Jim's. It was like him. Quietness and value--the description applied to both. Twenty-one dollars they took from her for it, and she hurried home with the 87 cents. With that chain on his watch Jim might be properly anxious about the time in any company. Grand as the watch was, he sometimes looked at it on the sly on account of the old leather strap that he used in place of a chain.

When Della reached home her intoxication gave way a little to prudence and reason. She got out her curling irons and lighted the gas and went to work repairing the ravages made by generosity added to love. Which is always a tremendous task, dear friends--a mammoth task.

Within forty minutes her head was covered with tiny, close-lying curls that made her look wonderfully like a truant schoolboy. She looked at her reflection in the mirror long, carefully, and critically.

"If Jim doesn't kill me," she said to herself, "before he takes a second look at me, he'll say I look like a Coney Island chorus girl. But what could I do--oh! what could I do with a dollar and eighty- seven cents?"

At 7 o'clock the coffee was made and the frying-pan was on the back of the stove hot and ready to cook the chops.

Jim was never late. Della doubled the fob chain in her hand and sat on the corner of the table near the door that he always entered. Then she heard his step on the stair away down on the first flight, and she turned white for just a moment. She had a habit for saying little silent prayer about the simplest everyday things, and now she whispered: "Please God, make him think I am still pretty."

The door opened and Jim stepped in and closed it. He looked thin and very serious. Poor fellow, he was only twenty-two--and to be burdened with a family! He needed a new overcoat and he was without gloves.

Jim stopped inside the door, as immovable as a setter at the scent of quail. His eyes were fixed upon Della, and there was an expression in them that she could not read, and it terrified her. It was not anger, nor surprise, nor disapproval, nor horror, nor any of the sentiments that she had been prepared for. He simply stared at her fixedly with that peculiar expression on his face.

Della wriggled off the table and went for him.

"Jim, darling," she cried, "don't look at me that way. I had my hair cut off and sold because I couldn't have lived through Christmas without giving you a present. It'll grow out again--you won't mind, will you? I just had to do it. My hair grows awfully fast. Say `Merry Christmas!' Jim, and let's be happy. You don't know what a nice-- what a beautiful, nice gift I've got for you."

"You've cut off your hair?" asked Jim, laboriously, as if he had not arrived at that patent fact yet even after the hardest mental labor.

"Cut it off and sold it," said Della. "Don't you like me just as well, anyhow? I'm me without my hair, ain't I?"

Jim looked about the room curiously.

"You say your hair is gone?" he said, with an air almost of idiocy.

"You needn't look for it," said Della. "It's sold, I tell you--sold and gone, too. It's Christmas Eve, boy. Be good to me, for it went for you. Maybe the hairs of my head were numbered," she went on with sudden serious sweetness, "but nobody could ever count my love for you. Shall I put the chops on, Jim?"

Out of his trance Jim seemed quickly to wake. He enfolded his Della. For ten seconds let us regard with discreet scrutiny some inconsequential object in the other direction. Eight dollars a week or a million a year--what is the difference? A mathematician or a wit would give you the wrong answer. The magi brought valuable gifts, but that was not among them. This dark assertion will be illuminated later on.

Jim drew a package from his overcoat pocket and threw it upon the table.

"Don't make any mistake, Dell," he said, "about me. I don't think there's anything in the way of a haircut or a shave or a shampoo that could make me like my girl any less. But if you'll unwrap that package you may see why you had me going a while at first."

White fingers and nimble tore at the string and paper. And then an ecstatic scream of joy; and then, alas! a quick feminine change to hysterical tears and wails, necessitating the immediate employment of all the comforting powers of the lord of the flat.

For there lay The Combs--the set of combs, side and back, that Della had worshipped long in a Broadway window. Beautiful combs, pure tortoise shell, with jewelled rims--just the shade to wear in the beautiful vanished hair. They were expensive combs, she knew, and her heart had simply craved and yearned over them without the least hope of possession. And now, they were hers, but the tresses that should have adorned the coveted adornments were gone.

But she hugged them to her bosom, and at length she was able to look up with dim eyes and a smile and say: "My hair grows so fast, Jim!"

And them Della leaped up like a little singed cat and cried, "Oh, oh!"

Jim had not yet seen his beautiful present. She held it out to him eagerly upon her open palm. The dull precious metal seemed to flash with a reflection of her bright and ardent spirit.

"Isn't it a dandy, Jim? I hunted all over town to find it. You'll have to look at the time a hundred times a day now. Give me your watch. I want to see how it looks on it."

Instead of obeying, Jim tumbled down on the couch and put his hands under the back of his head and smiled.

"Dell," said he, "let's put our Christmas presents away and keep 'em a while. They're too nice to use just at present. I sold the watch to get the money to buy your combs. And now suppose you put the chops on."

The magi, as you know, were wise men--wonderfully wise men--who brought gifts to the Babe in the manger. They invented the art of giving Christmas presents. Being wise, their gifts were no doubt wise ones, possibly bearing the privilege of exchange in case of duplication. And here I have lamely related to you the uneventful chronicle of two foolish children in a flat who most unwisely sacrificed for each other the greatest treasures of their house. But in a last word to the wise of these days let it be said that of all who give gifts these two were the wisest. O all who give and receive gifts, such as they are wisest. Everywhere they are wisest. They are the magi.

'Papa Panov's Special Christmas'

By

Leo Tolstoy

It was Christmas Eve and although it was still afternoon, lights had begun to appear in the shops and houses of the little Russian village, for the short winter day was nearly over. Excited children scurried indoors and now only muffled sounds of chatter and laughter escaped from closed shutters.

Old Papa Panov, the village shoemaker, stepped outside his shop to take one last look around. The sounds of happiness, the bright lights and the faint but delicious smells of Christmas cooking reminded him of past Christmas times when his wife had still been alive and his own children little. Now they had gone. His usually cheerful face, with the little laughter wrinkles behind the round steel spectacles, looked sad now. But he went back indoors with a firm step, put up the shutters and set a pot of coffee to heat on the charcoal stove. Then, with a sigh, he settled in his big armchair.

Papa Panov did not often read, but tonight he pulled down the big old family Bible and, slowly tracing the lines with one forefinger, he read again the Christmas story. He read how Mary and Joseph, tired by their journey to Bethlehem, found no room for them at the inn, so that Mary's little baby was born in the cowshed.

"Oh, dear, oh, dear!" exclaimed Papa Panov, "if only they had come here! I would have given them my bed and I could have covered the baby with my patchwork quilt to keep him warm.

He read on about the wise men who had come to see the baby Jesus, bringing him splendid gifts. Papa Panov's face fell. "I have no gift that I could give him," he thought sadly.

Then his face brightened. He put down the Bible, got up and stretched his long arms t the shelf high up in his little room. He took down a small, dusty box and opened it. Inside was a perfect pair of tiny leather shoes. Papa Panov smiled with satisfaction. Yes, they were as good as he had remembered- the best shoes he had ever made. "I should give him those," he decided, as he gently put them away and sat down again.

He was feeling tired now, and the further he read the sleeper he became. The print began to dance before his eyes so that he closed them, just for a minute. In no time at all Papa Panov was fast asleep.

And as he slept he dreamed. He dreamed that someone was in his room and he know at once, as one does in dreams, who the person was. It was Jesus.

"You have been wishing that you could see me, Papa Panov." he said kindly, "then look for me tomorrow. It will be Christmas Day and I will visit you. But look carefully, for I shall not tell you who I am."

When at last Papa Panov awoke, the bells were ringing out and a thin light was filtering through the shutters. "Bless my soul!" said Papa Panov. "It's Christmas Day!"

He stood up and stretched himself for he was rather stiff. Then his face filled with happiness as he remembered his dream. This would be a very special Christmas after all, for Jesus was coming to visit him. How would he look? Would he be a little baby, as at that first Christmas? Would he be a grown man, a carpenter- or the great King that he is, God's Son? He must watch carefully the whole day through so that he recognized him however he came.

Papa Panov put on a special pot of coffee for his Christmas breakfast, took down the shutters and looked out of the window. The street was deserted, no one was stirring yet. No one except the road sweeper. He looked as miserable and dirty as ever, and well he might! Whoever wanted to work on Christmas Day - and in the raw cold and bitter freezing mist of such a morning?

Papa Panov opened the shop door, letting in a thin stream of cold air. "Come in!" he shouted across the street cheerily. "Come in and have some hot coffee to keep out the cold!"

The sweeper looked up, scarcely able to believe his ears. He was only too glad to put down his broom and come into the warm room. His old clothes steamed gently in the heat of the stove and he clasped both red hands round the comforting warm mug as he drank.

Papa Panov watched him with satisfaction, but every now and them his eyes strayed to the window. It would never do to miss his special visitor.

"Expecting someone?" the sweeper asked at last. So Papa Panov told him about his dream.

"Well, I hope he comes," the sweeper said, "you've given me a bit of Christmas cheer I never expected to have. I'd say you deserve to have your dream come true." And he actually smiled.

When he had gone, Papa Panov put on cabbage soup for his dinner, then went to the door again, scanning the street. He saw no one. But he was mistaken. Someone was coming.

The girl walked so slowly and quietly, hugging the walls of shops and houses, that it was a while before he noticed her. She looked very tired and she was carrying something. As she drew nearer he could see that it was a baby, wrapped in a thin shawl. There was such sadness in her face and in the pinched little face of the baby, that Papa Panov's heart went out to them.

"Won't you come in," he called, stepping outside to meet them. "You both need a warm by the fire and a rest."

The young mother let him shepherd her indoors and to the comfort of the armchair. She gave a big sigh of relief.

"I'll warm some milk for the baby," Papa Panov said, "I've had children of my own- I can feed her for you." He took the milk from the stove and carefully fed the baby from a spoon, warming her tiny feet by the stove at the same time.

"She needs shoes," the cobbler said.

But the girl replied, "I can't afford shoes, I've got no husband to bring home money. I'm on my way to the next village to get work."

Sudden thought flashed through Papa Panov's mind. He remembered the little shoes he had looked at last night. But he had been keeping those for Jesus. He looked again at the cold little feet and made up his mind.

"Try these on her," he said, handing the baby and the shoes to the mother. The beautiful little shoes were a perfect fit. The girl smiled happily and the baby gurgled with pleasure.

"You have been so kind to us," the girl said, when she got up with her baby to go. "May all your Christmas wishes come true!"

But Papa Panov was beginning to wonder if his very special Christmas wish would come true. Perhaps he had missed his visitor? He looked anxiously up and down the street. There were plenty of people about but they were all faces that he recognized. There were neighbors going to call on their families. They nodded and smiled and wished him Happy Christmas! Or beggars- and Papa Panov hurried indoors to fetch them hot soup and a generous hunk of bread, hurrying out again in case he missed the Important Stranger.

All too soon the winter dusk fell. When Papa Panov next went to the door and strained his eyes, he could no longer make out the passers-by. most were home and indoors by now anyway. He walked slowly back into his room at last, put up the shutters, and sat down wearily in his armchair.

So it had been just a dream after all. Jesus had not come.

Then all at once he knew that he was no longer alone in the room.

This was not dream for he was wide awake. At first he seemed to see before his eyes the long stream of people who had come to him that day. He saw again the old road sweeper, the young mother and her baby and the beggars he had fed. As they passed, each whispered, "Didn't you see me, Papa Panov?"

"Who are you?" he called out, bewildered.

Then another voice answered him. It was the voice from his dream- the voice of Jesus.

"I was hungry and you fed me," he said. "I was naked and you clothed me. I was cold and you warmed me. I came to you today in everyone of those you helped and welcomed."

Then all was quiet and still. Only the sound of the big clock ticking. A great peace and happiness seemed to fill the room, overflowing Papa Panov's heart until he wanted to burst out singing and laughing and dancing with joy.

"So he did come after all!" was all that he said.

The Elves and the Shoemaker

By

Brothers Grimm

A shoemaker, by no fault of his own, had become so poor that at last he had nothing left but leather for one pair of shoes. So in the evening, he cut out the shoes which he wished to begin to make the next morning, and as he had a good conscience, he lay down quietly in his bed, commended himself to God, and fell asleep. In the morning, after he had said his prayers, and was just going to sit down to work, the two shoes stood quite finished on his table. He was astounded, and knew not what to say to it. He took the shoes in his hands to observe them closer, and they were so neatly made that there was not one bad stitch in them, just as if they were intended as a masterpiece.

Soon after, a buyer came in, and as the shoes pleased him so well, he paid more for them than was customary, and, with the money, the shoemaker was able to purchase leather for two pairs of shoes. He cut them out at night, and next morning was about to set to work with fresh courage; but he had no need to do so, for, when he got up, they were already made, and buyers also were not wanting, who gave him money enough to buy leather for four pairs of shoes. The following morning, too, he found the four pairs made; and so it went on constantly — what he cut out in the evening was finished by the morning, so that he soon had his honest independence again, and at last became a wealthy man.

Now it befell that one evening not long before Christmas, when the man had been cutting out, he said to his wife, before going to bed, "What think you if we were to stay up to-night to see who it is that lends us this helping hand?" The woman liked the idea, and lighted a candle, and then they hid themselves in a corner of the room, behind some clothes which were hanging up there, and watched. When it was midnight, two pretty little naked men came, sat down by the shoemaker's table, took all the work which was cut out before them and began to stitch, and sew, and hammer so skilfully and so quickly with their little fingers that the shoemaker could not turn away his eyes for astonishment. They did not stop until all was done, and stood finished on the table; and then they ran quickly away.

Next morning the woman said, "The little men have made us rich, and we really must show that we are grateful for it. They run about so, and have nothing on, and must be cold. I'll tell thee what I'll do: I will make them little shirts, and coats, and vests, and trousers, and knit both of them a pair of stockings, and do thou, too, make them two little pairs of shoes." The man said, "I shall be very glad to do it;" and one night, when everything was ready, they laid their presents all together on the table instead of the cut-out work, and then concealed themselves to see how the little men would behave. At midnight they came bounding in, and wanted to get to work at once, but as they did not find any leather cut out, but only the pretty little articles of clothing, they were at first astonished, and then they showed intense delight. They dressed themselves with the greatest rapidity, putting the pretty clothes on, and singing,

> "Now we are boys so fine to see,
> Why should we longer cobblers be?"

Then they danced and skipped and leapt over chairs and benches. At last they danced out of doors. From that time forth they came no more, but as long as the shoemaker lived all went well with him, and all his undertakings prospered.

How the Fir Tree Became the Christmas Tree

By

Aunt Hede

This is the story of how the fir tree became the Christmas tree.

At the time when the Christ Child was born all the people, the animals, and the trees, and plants were very happy. The Child was born to bring peace and happiness to the whole world. People came daily to see the little One, and they always brought gifts with them.

There were three trees standing near the crypt which saw the people, and they wished that they, too, might give presents to the Christ Child.

The Palm said: "I will choose my most beautiful leaf, and place it as a fan over the Child."

"And I," said the Olive, "will sprinkle sweet-smelling oil upon His head."

"What can I give to the Child?" asked the Fir, who stood near.

"You!" cried the others. "You have nothing to offer Him. Your needles would prick Him, and your tears are sticky."

So the poor little Fir tree was very unhappy, and it said: "Yes, you are right. I have nothing to offer the Christ Child."

Now, quite near the trees stood the Christmas Angel, who had heard all that the trees had said. The Angel was sorry for the Fir tree who was so lowly and without envy of the other trees. So, when it was dark, and the stars came out, he begged a few of the little stars to come down and rest upon the branches of the Fir tree. They did as the Christmas Angel asked, and the Fir tree shone suddenly with a beautiful light.

And, at that very moment, the Christ Child opened His eyes—for He had been asleep—and as the lovely light fell upon Him He smiled.

Every year people keep the dear Christmas Child's birthday by giving gifts to each other, and every year, in remembrance of His first birthday, the Christmas Angel places in every house a fir tree, also. Covered with starry candles it shines for the children as the stars shone for the Christ Child. The Fir tree was rewarded for its meekness, for to no other tree is it given to shine upon so many happy faces.

A Kidnapped Santa Claus

By

L. Frank Baum

Santa Claus lives in the Laughing Valley, where stands the big, rambling castle in which his toys are manufactured. His workmen, selected from the ryls, knooks, pixies and fairies, live with him, and every one is as busy as can be from one year's end to another.

It is called the Laughing Valley because everything there is happy and gay. The brook chuckles to itself as it leaps rollicking between its green banks; the wind whistles merrily in the trees; the sunbeams dance lightly over the soft grass, and the violets and wild flowers look smilingly up from their green nests. To laugh one needs to be happy; to be happy one needs to be content. And throughout the Laughing Valley of Santa Claus contentment reigns supreme.

On one side is the mighty Forest of Burzee. At the other side stands the huge mountain that contains the Caves of the Daemons. And between them the Valley lies smiling and peaceful.

One would think that our good old Santa Claus, who devotes his days to making children happy, would have no enemies on all the earth; and, as a matter of fact, for a long period of time he encountered nothing but love wherever he might go.

But the Daemons who live in the mountain caves grew to hate Santa Claus very much, and all for the simple reason that he made children happy.

The Caves of the Daemons are five in number. A broad pathway leads up to the first cave, which is a finely arched cavern at the foot of the mountain, the entrance being beautifully carved and decorated. In it resides the Daemon of Selfishness. Back of this is another cavern inhabited by the Daemon of Envy. The cave of the Daemon of Hatred is next in order, and through this one passes to the home of the Daemon of Malice--situated in a dark and fearful cave in the very heart of the mountain. I do not know what lies beyond this. Some say there are terrible pitfalls leading to death and destruction, and this may very well be true. However, from each one of the four caves mentioned there is a small, narrow tunnel leading to the fifth cave--a cozy little room occupied by the Daemon of Repentance. And as the rocky floors of these passages are well worn by the track of passing feet, I judge that many wanderers in the Caves of the Daemons have escaped through the tunnels to the abode of the Daemon of Repentance, who is said to be a pleasant sort of fellow who gladly opens for one a little door admitting you into fresh air and sunshine again.

Well, these Daemons of the Caves, thinking they had great cause to dislike old Santa Claus, held a meeting one day to discuss the matter.

"I'm really getting lonesome," said the Daemon of Selfishness. "For Santa Claus distributes so many pretty Christmas gifts to all the children that they become happy and generous, through his example, and keep away from my cave."

"I'm having the same trouble," rejoined the Daemon of Envy. "The little ones seem quite content with Santa Claus, and there are few, indeed, that I can coax to become envious."

"And that makes it bad for me!" declared the Daemon of Hatred. "For if no children pass through the Caves of Selfishness and Envy, none can get to MY cavern."

"Or to mine," added the Daemon of Malice.

"For my part," said the Daemon of Repentance, "it is easily seen that if children do not visit your caves they have no need to visit mine; so that I am quite as neglected as you are."

"And all because of this person they call Santa Claus!" exclaimed the Daemon of Envy. "He is simply ruining our business, and something must be done at once."

To this they readily agreed; but what to do was another and more difficult matter to settle. They knew that Santa Claus worked all through the year at his castle in the Laughing Valley, preparing the gifts he was to distribute on Christmas Eve; and at first they resolved to try to tempt him into their caves, that they might lead him on to the terrible pitfalls that ended in destruction.

So the very next day, while Santa Claus was busily at work, surrounded by his little band of assistants, the Daemon of Selfishness came to him and said:

"These toys are wonderfully bright and pretty. Why do you not keep them for yourself? It's a pity to give them to those noisy boys and fretful girls, who break and destroy them so quickly."

"Nonsense!" cried the old graybeard, his bright eyes twinkling merrily as he turned toward the tempting Daemon. "The boys and girls are never so noisy and fretful after receiving my presents, and if I can make them happy for one day in the year I am quite content."

So the Daemon went back to the others, who awaited him in their caves, and said:

"I have failed, for Santa Claus is not at all selfish."

The following day the Daemon of Envy visited Santa Claus. Said he: "The toy shops are full of playthings quite as pretty as those you are making. What a shame it is that they should interfere with your business! They make toys by machinery much quicker than you can make them by hand; and they sell them for money, while you get nothing at all for your work."

But Santa Claus refused to be envious of the toy shops.

"I can supply the little ones but once a year--on Christmas Eve," he answered; "for the children are many, and I am but one. And as my work is one of love and kindness I would be ashamed to receive money for my little gifts. But throughout all the year the children must be amused in some way, and so the toy shops are able to bring much happiness to my little friends. I like the toy shops, and am glad to see them prosper."

In spite of the second rebuff, the Daemon of Hatred thought he would try to influence Santa Claus. So the next day he entered the busy workshop and said:

"Good morning, Santa! I have bad news for you."

"Then run away, like a good fellow," answered Santa Claus. "Bad news is something that should be kept secret and never told."

"You cannot escape this, however," declared the Daemon; "for in the world are a good many who do not believe in Santa Claus, and these you are bound to hate bitterly, since they have so wronged you."

"Stuff and rubbish!" cried Santa.

"And there are others who resent your making children happy and who sneer at you and call you a foolish old rattlepate! You are quite right to hate such base slanderers, and you ought to be revenged upon them for their evil words."

"But I don't hate 'em!" exclaimed Santa Claus positively. "Such people do me no real harm, but merely render themselves and their children unhappy. Poor things! I'd much rather help them any day than injure them."

Indeed, the Daemons could not tempt old Santa Claus in any way. On the contrary, he was shrewd enough to see that their object in visiting him was to make mischief and trouble, and his cheery laughter disconcerted the evil ones and showed to them the folly of such an undertaking. So they abandoned honeyed words and determined to use force.

It was well known that no harm can come to Santa Claus while he is in the Laughing Valley, for the fairies, and ryls, and knooks all protect him. But on Christmas Eve he drives his reindeer out into the big world, carrying a sleighload of toys and pretty gifts to the children; and this was the time and the occasion when his enemies had the best chance to injure him. So the Daemons laid their plans and awaited the arrival of Christmas Eve.

The moon shone big and white in the sky, and the snow lay crisp and sparkling on the ground as Santa Claus cracked his whip and sped away out of the Valley into the great world beyond. The roomy sleigh was packed full with huge sacks of toys, and as the reindeer dashed onward our jolly old Santa laughed and whistled and sang for very joy. For in all his merry life this was the one day in the year when he was happiest--the day he lovingly bestowed the treasures of his workshop upon the little children.

It would be a busy night for him, he well knew. As he whistled and shouted and cracked his whip again, he reviewed in mind all the towns and cities and farmhouses where he was expected, and figured that he had just enough presents to go around and make every child happy. The reindeer knew exactly what was expected of them, and dashed along so swiftly that their feet scarcely seemed to touch the snow-covered ground.

Suddenly a strange thing happened: a rope shot through the moonlight and a big noose that was in the end of it settled over the arms and body of Santa Claus and drew tight. Before he could resist or even cry out he was jerked from the seat of the sleigh and tumbled head foremost into a snowbank, while the reindeer rushed onward with the load of toys and carried it quickly out of sight and sound.

Such a surprising experience confused old Santa for a moment, and when he had collected his senses he found that the wicked Daemons had pulled him from the snowdrift and bound him tightly with many coils of the stout rope. And then they carried the kidnapped Santa Claus away to their mountain, where they thrust the prisoner into a secret cave and chained him to the rocky wall so that he could not escape.

"Ha, ha!" laughed the Daemons, rubbing their hands together with cruel glee. "What will the children do now? How they will cry and scold and storm when they find there are no toys in their stockings and no gifts on their Christmas trees! And what a lot of punishment they will receive from their parents, and how they will flock to our Caves of Selfishness, and Envy, and Hatred, and Malice! We have done a mighty clever thing, we Daemons of the Caves!"

Now it so chanced that on this Christmas Eve the good Santa Claus had taken with him in his sleigh Nuter the Ryl, Peter the Knook, Kilter the Pixie, and a small fairy named Wisk--his four favorite assistants. These little people he had often found very useful in helping him to distribute his gifts to the children, and when their master was so suddenly dragged from the sleigh they were all snugly tucked underneath the seat, where the sharp wind could not reach them.

The tiny immortals knew nothing of the capture of Santa Claus until some time after he had disappeared. But finally they missed his cheery voice, and as their master always sang or whistled on his journeys, the silence warned them that something was wrong.

Little Wisk stuck out his head from underneath the seat and found Santa Claus gone and no one to direct the flight of the reindeer.

"Whoa!" he called out, and the deer obediently slackened speed and came to a halt.

Peter and Nuter and Kilter all jumped upon the seat and looked back over the track made by the sleigh. But Santa Claus had been left miles and miles behind.

"What shall we do?" asked Wisk anxiously, all the mirth and mischief banished from his wee face by this great calamity.

"We must go back at once and find our master," said Nuter the Ryl, who thought and spoke with much deliberation.

"No, no!" exclaimed Peter the Knook, who, cross and crabbed though he was, might always be depended upon in an emergency. "If we delay, or go back, there will not be time to get the toys to the children before morning; and that would grieve Santa Claus more than anything else."

"It is certain that some wicked creatures have captured him," added Kilter thoughtfully, "and their object must be to make the children unhappy. So our first duty is to get the toys distributed as carefully as if Santa Claus were himself present. Afterward we can search for our master and easily secure his freedom."

This seemed such good and sensible advice that the others at once resolved to adopt it. So Peter the Knook called to the reindeer, and the faithful animals again sprang forward and dashed over hill and valley, through forest and plain, until they came to the houses wherein children lay sleeping and dreaming of the pretty gifts they would find on Christmas morning.

The little immortals had set themselves a difficult task; for although they had assisted Santa Claus on many of his journeys, their master had always directed and guided them and told them exactly what he wished them to do. But now they had to distribute the toys according to their own judgment, and they did not understand children as well as did old Santa. So it is no wonder they made some laughable errors.

Mamie Brown, who wanted a doll, got a drum instead; and a drum is of no use to a girl who loves dolls. And Charlie Smith, who delights to romp and play out of doors, and who wanted some new rubber boots to keep his feet dry, received a sewing box filled with colored worsteds and threads and needles, which made him so provoked that he thoughtlessly called our dear Santa Claus a fraud.

Had there been many such mistakes the Daemons would have accomplished their evil purpose and made the children unhappy. But the little friends of the absent Santa Claus labored faithfully and intelligently to carry out their master's ideas, and they made fewer errors than might be expected under such unusual circumstances.

And, although they worked as swiftly as possible, day had begun to break before the toys and other presents were all distributed; so for the first time in many years the reindeer trotted into the Laughing Valley, on their return, in broad daylight, with the brilliant sun peeping over the edge of the forest to prove they were far behind their accustomed hours.

Having put the deer in the stable, the little folk began to wonder how they might rescue their master; and they realized they must discover, first of all, what had happened to him and where he was.

So Wisk the Fairy transported himself to the bower of the Fairy Queen, which was located deep in the heart of the Forest of Burzee; and once there, it did not take him long to find out all about the naughty Daemons and how they had kidnapped the good Santa Claus to prevent his making children happy. The Fairy Queen also promised her assistance, and then, fortified by this powerful support, Wisk flew back to where Nuter and Peter and Kilter awaited him, and the four counseled together and laid plans to rescue their master from his enemies.

It is possible that Santa Claus was not as merry as usual during the night that succeeded his capture. For although he had faith in the judgment of his little friends he could not avoid a certain amount of worry, and an anxious look would creep at times into his kind old eyes as he thought of the disappointment that might await his dear little children. And the Daemons, who guarded him by turns, one after another, did not neglect to taunt him with contemptuous words in his helpless condition.

When Christmas Day dawned the Daemon of Malice was guarding the prisoner, and his tongue was sharper than that of any of the others.

"The children are waking up, Santa!" he cried. "They are waking up to find their stockings empty! Ho, ho! How they will quarrel, and wail, and stamp their feet in anger! Our caves will be full today, old Santa! Our caves are sure to be full!"

But to this, as to other like taunts, Santa Claus answered nothing. He was much grieved by his capture, it is true; but his courage did not forsake him. And, finding that the prisoner would not reply to his jeers, the Daemon of Malice presently went away, and sent the Daemon of Repentance to take his place.

This last personage was not so disagreeable as the others. He had gentle and refined features, and his voice was soft and pleasant in tone.

"My brother Daemons do not trust me overmuch," said he, as he entered the cavern; "but it is morning, now, and the mischief is done. You cannot visit the children again for another year."

"That is true," answered Santa Claus, almost cheerfully; "Christmas Eve is past, and for the first time in centuries I have not visited my children."

"The little ones will be greatly disappointed," murmured the Daemon of Repentance, almost regretfully; "but that cannot be helped now. Their grief is likely to make the children selfish and envious and hateful, and if they come to the Caves of the Daemons today I shall get a chance to lead some of them to my Cave of Repentance."

"Do you never repent, yourself?" asked Santa Claus, curiously.

"Oh, yes, indeed," answered the Daemon. "I am even now repenting that I assisted in your capture. Of course it is too late to remedy the evil that has been done; but repentance, you know, can come only after an evil thought or deed, for in the beginning there is nothing to repent of."

"So I understand," said Santa Claus. "Those who avoid evil need never visit your cave."

"As a rule, that is true," replied the Daemon; "yet you, who have done no evil, are about to visit my cave at once; for to prove that I sincerely regret my share in your capture I am going to permit you to escape."

This speech greatly surprised the prisoner, until he reflected that it was just what might be expected of the Daemon of Repentance. The fellow at once busied himself untying the knots that bound Santa Claus and unlocking the chains that fastened him to the wall. Then he led the way through a long tunnel until they both emerged in the Cave of Repentance.

"I hope you will forgive me," said the Daemon pleadingly. "I am not really a bad person, you know; and I believe I accomplish a great deal of good in the world."

With this he opened a back door that let in a flood of sunshine, and Santa Claus sniffed the fresh air gratefully.

"I bear no malice," said he to the Daemon, in a gentle voice; "and I am sure the world would be a dreary place without you. So, good morning, and a Merry Christmas to you!"

With these words he stepped out to greet the bright morning, and a moment later he was trudging along, whistling softly to himself, on his way to his home in the Laughing Valley.

Marching over the snow toward the mountain was a vast army, made up of the most curious creatures imaginable. There were numberless knooks from the forest, as rough and crooked in appearance as the gnarled branches of the trees they ministered to. And there were dainty ryls from the fields, each one bearing the emblem of the flower or plant it guarded. Behind these were many ranks of pixies, gnomes and nymphs, and in the rear a thousand beautiful fairies floated along in gorgeous array.

This wonderful army was led by Wisk, Peter, Nuter, and Kilter, who had assembled it to rescue Santa Claus from captivity and to punish the Daemons who had dared to take him away from his beloved children.

And, although they looked so bright and peaceful, the little immortals were armed with powers that would be very terrible to those who had incurred their anger. Woe to the Daemons of the Caves if this mighty army of vengeance ever met them!

But lo! coming to meet his loyal friends appeared the imposing form of Santa Claus, his white beard floating in the breeze and his bright eyes sparkling with pleasure at this proof of the love and veneration he had inspired in the hearts of the most powerful creatures in existence.

And while they clustered around him and danced with glee at his safe return, he gave them earnest thanks for their support. But Wisk, and Nuter, and Peter, and Kilter, he embraced affectionately.

"It is useless to pursue the Daemons," said Santa Claus to the army. "They have their place in the world, and can never be destroyed. But that is a great pity, nevertheless," he continued musingly.

So the fairies, and knooks, and pixies, and ryls all escorted the good man to his castle, and there left him to talk over the events of the night with his little assistants.

Wisk had already rendered himself invisible and flown through the big world to see how the children were getting along on this bright Christmas morning; and by the time he returned, Peter had finished telling Santa Claus of how they had distributed the toys.

"We really did very well," cried the fairy, in a pleased voice; "for I found little unhappiness among the children this morning. Still, you must not get captured again, my dear master; for we might not be so fortunate another time in carrying out your ideas."

He then related the mistakes that had been made, and which he had not discovered until his tour of inspection. And Santa Claus at once sent him with rubber boots for Charlie Smith, and a doll for Mamie Brown; so that even those two disappointed ones became happy.

As for the wicked Daemons of the Caves, they were filled with anger and chagrin when they found that their clever capture of Santa Claus had come to naught. Indeed, no one on that Christmas Day appeared to be at all selfish, or envious, or hateful. And, realizing that while the children's saint had so many powerful friends it was folly to oppose him, the Daemons never again attempted to interfere with his journeys on Christmas Eve.

The Holy Night

By

Selma Lagerlöf

There was a man who went out in the dark night to borrow live coals to kindle a fire. He went from hut to hut and knocked. "Dear friends, help me!" said he. "My wife has just given birth to a child, and I must make a fire to warm her and the little one."

But it was way in the night, and all the people were asleep. No one replied.

The man walked and walked. At last he saw the gleam of a fire a long way off. Then he went in that direction and saw that the fire was burning in the open. A lot of sheep were were sleeping around the fire, and an old shepherd sat and watched over the flock.

When the man who wanted to borrow fire came up to the sheep, he saw that three big dogs lay asleep at the shepherd's feet. All three awoke when the man approached and opened their great jaws, as though they wanted to bark; but not a sound was heard. The man noticed that the hair on their backs stood up and that their sharp, white teeth glistened in the firelight. They dashed toward him.

He felt that one of them bit at his leg and one at this hand and that one clung to this throat. But their jaws and teeth wouldn't obey them, and the man didn't suffer the least harm.

Now the man wished to go farther, to get what he needed. But the sheep lay back to back and so close to one another that he couldn't pass them. Then the man stepped upon their backs and walked over them and up to the fire. And not one of the animals awoke or moved.

When the man had almost reached the fire, the shepherd looked up. He was a surly old man, who was unfriendly and harsh toward human beings. And when he saw the strange man coming, he seized the long, spiked staff, which he always held in his hand when he tended his flock, and threw it at him. The staff came right toward the man, but, before it reached him, it turned off to one side and whizzed past him, far out in the meadow.

Now the man came up to the shepherd and said to him: "Good man, help me, and lend me a little fire! My wife has just given birth to a child, and I must make a fire to warm her and the little one."

The shepherd would rather have said no, but when he pondered that the dogs couldn't hurt the man, and the sheep had not run from him, and that the staff had not wished to strike him, he was a little afraid, and dared not deny the man that which he asked.

"Take as much as you need!" he said to the man.

But then the fire was nearly burnt out. There were no logs or branches left, only a big heap of live coals, and the stranger had neither spade nor shovel wherein he could carry the red-hot coals.

When the shepherd saw this, he said again: "Take as much as you need!" And he was glad that the man wouldn't be able to take away any coals.

But the man stopped and picked coals from the ashes with his bare hands, and laid them in his mantle. And he didn't burn his hands when he touched them, nor did the coals scorch his mantle; but he carried them away as if they had been nuts or apples.

And when the shepherd, who was such a cruel and hardhearted man, saw all this, he began to wonder to himself. What kind of a night is this, when the dogs do not bite, the sheep are not scared, the staff does not kill, or the fire scorch? He called the stranger back and said to him: "What kind of a night is this? And how does it happen that all things show you compassion?"

Then said the man: "I cannot tell you if you yourself do not see it." And he wished to go his way, that he might soon make a fire and warm his wife and child.

But the shepherd did not wish to lose sight of the man before he had found out what all this might portend. He got up and followed the man till they came to the place where he lived.

Then the shepherd saw the man didn't have so much as a hut to dwell in, but that his wife and babe were lying in a mountain grotto, where there was nothing except the cold and naked stone walls.

But the shepherd thought that perhaps the poor innocent child might freeze to death there in the grotto; and, although he was a hard man, he was touched, and thought he would like to help it. And he loosened the knapsack from his shoulder, took from it a soft white sheepskin, gave it to the strange man, and said that he should let the child sleep on it.

But just as soon as he showed that he, too, could be merciful, his eyes were opened, and he saw what he had not been able to see before, and heard what he could not have heard before.

He saw that all around him stood a ring of little silver-winged angels, and each held a stringed instrument, and all sang in loud tones that tonight the Saviour was born who should redeem the world from its sins.

Then he understood how all things were so happy this night that they didn't want to do anything wrong.

And it was not only around the shepherd that there were angels, but he saw them everywhere. They sat inside the grotto, they sat outside on the mountain, and they flew under the heavens. They came marching in great companies, and, as they passed, they paused and cast a glance at the child.

There was such jubilation and such gladness and songs and play! And all this he saw in the dark night whereas before he could not have made out anything. He was so happy because his eyes had been opened that he fell upon his knees and thanked God.

What that shepherd saw, we might also see, for the angels fly down from heaven every Christmas Eve, if we could only see them.

You must remember this, for it is as true, as true as that I see you and you see me. It is not revealed by the light of lamps or candles, and it does not depend upon sun and moon; but that which is needful is that we have such eyes as can see God's glory.

The Magi in the West and Their Search for the Christ

A Tale for the Christmas-Tide

By

Frederick E. Dewhurst

The Mountain of Vision

Now, it happened a long time ago, in the year ——, but the exact year does not matter, because you will not find this story written in the history of any of the nations of the world. But in one of the countries of Europe bordering on the Mediterranean Sea was a lofty mountain, which, to the dwellers in the plains below, seemed to reach to the very sky. At times its summit was covered with clouds, so that it could not be seen; at other times it stood out fair and clear, as though silently asking the people to look up and not down. The lower slopes of the mountain were covered with olive trees, with groves of oranges and lemons, and with vineyards, and they were dotted here and there with the little white cottages of the peasants who made their living from these groves and vineyards, the fruit of which they sold in the city not far away.

Sunset in the Sea

Along the mountain-side wound a foot-trail even to the summit, and nowhere, in all the region, was there a finer view of the Mediterranean than from the summit of this mountain. In the long summer afternoons the peasants and children would climb to the top and look off on the lovely picture of land and sea. Then they would eat their simple lunch of bread and dates and olives and quench their thirst from the spring on the mountain-side, which they called "Dew-of-heaven," so clear and fresh and sparkling was it; and when the sun began to touch the western sky with his pencils of gold and carmine and purple, they hastened down, that they might reach their cottages before the night shut in.

A Stranger Cometh

On the day when this story begins a man was standing on the summit of the mountain looking across the sea in the direction where you will find Tyre and Joppa on the map. He was, very plainly, not one of the peasants who lived on the mountain-side. He looked about sixty years of age; he was tall and erect, though he carried a staff in his hand. His hair and beard were long and flowing, and almost gray, but his eye was clear and penetrating, and he was looking across the sea as though he expected some one to appear.

And while he stood there gazing seaward, there appeared a second man on the summit, helping himself up with his staff, and panting with the effort of the long climb. From his dress and manner it was plain that this man, too, was not one of the peasants, for, like the first comer, he seemed to belong to another age and clime. The two men glanced at each other and gave such greeting as strangers might who should meet in so solitary a spot as a mountain summit. Then both lapsed into silence and looked off across the sea.

And Findeth a Friend

Presently the last comer seemed to awake from his reverie. He walked over to the place where the other man was sitting, still gazing off toward Joppa, and touched him on the shoulder: "A thousand pardons, my friend," he said, "but my mind is haunted with some far-off recollection, as though in some other land and some far-off time I had seen thy face. Wilt thou have the kindness to tell me thy name?"

Without lifting his eyes from the sea, and in a tone which seemed regretful and sad, the stranger replied: "My name is Gaspard."

A Far-off Pilgrimage Recalled

"Gaspard! Indeed, then have I seen thee! Look at me, my friend; dost thou not remember me? My name is Melchoir. Dost thou not recall that time, how long I know not, when thou and I and Balthazar followed a star which led us to a little Jewish hamlet, thou bearing gold and I frankincense, and Balthazar myrrh? Dost thou not remember how, on the long journey thither, we talked about the young Prince, whom we expected to find in a royal palace, and how at last when we reached the village, following the star, we were led not to a palace but to a little inn, and not even to a room within the inn, but to the stable-yard, where we found a sweet-faced woman bending over a babe cradled in a manger; and standing near, a sturdy peasant, proud and happy, whose name was Joseph? Dost thou not remember, too, that when we had recovered from our surprise, we left our gifts and greetings, and went our way as men who had been dreaming? Gaspard, dost thou not remember?"

And Wanderings in Many Lands

And Gaspard, looking now intently in the other's face, replied: "Yes, Melchoir, I remember thee, and I remember the journey of which thou hast spoken better than I remember aught else. Neither have I forgotten the surprise and disappointment with which we came to the place whither the star led us; nor how, after leaving our gifts, we went away as in a dream; and, Melchoir, I have been dreaming ever since. Even here hast thou found me in a dream of perplexity. I am still Gaspard, the wandering magician; for how many years I know not, I have wandered up and down these lands of Europe. I have crossed the seas; in every place I have sought to find the kingdom over which we were told this young prince was one day to reign. Dost thou not remember that we were told His kingdom was to last forever, that He would reign in it himself forever and would never die? Alas! I have lost the old power of the magician's art. I can summon no star to guide me to the place where I shall find this kingdom and its king."

If Only Balthazar Were Here

"Truly, Gaspard," answered Melchoir, "the story of your wanderings is but the repetition of my own; and even now was I drawn to this mountain summit on the self-same errand that brought you here,—to see if I could not discover in the direction of yonder land, where Bethlehem was, some star which might prove to be His star, and which might guide me in the new quest. If only our old companion, Balthazar, were with us now, he might give us the clew to our search, for not only was he more skilful in the magician's art, but he was braver and more courageous, and withal more serene in spirit."

A Song in the Air

Now, even while Melchoir was speaking, a voice was heard a little way down the mountain. Gaspard and Melchoir stopped to listen. The voice was singing, and the words of the song floated up to them distinctly:

If the sun has hid its light, If the day has turned to night, If the heavens are not benign, If the stars refuse to shine—
Heart of man lose not thy hope; Door, there's none that shall not ope; Path, there's none that shall not clear; Heart of man! why shouldst thou fear?

If for years should be thy quest, If for years thou hast no rest, If thou circlest earth and sea, If thou worn and weary be—
Heart of man, lose not thy hope; Door, there's none that shall not ope; Path, there's none that shall not clear; Heart of man! why shouldst thou fear?
Balthazar Cometh

"That," exclaimed Gaspard and Melchoir together, "is the voice of Balthazar," and they hastened to meet him, for he was now almost at the summit, and the refrain of his song was still upon his lips. At that moment Balthazar sprang up from the sloping path into full view of the two men, and, giving each a hand, exclaimed: "Gaspard, Melchoir, beloved companions, I have found you at last. The peasants below were not mistaken. From their description, I was certain I should find you here. And you, too, have been searching these long years for the kingdom of the Christ! and, like me, you have met with disappointment; but, comrades, be not of faint heart:

Door, there's none that shall not ope; Path, there's none that shall not clear.

Let us hasten down the mountain, for see! the sky is already growing gold and crimson beyond the pillars of Hercules. Let us seek the wayfarer's lodging with the hospitable peasants in the valley, and tomorrow let us begin our search for the Christ anew. We have wandered alone; let us invoke now the star to guide us together."

Forget Not Hospitality

That night, therefore, the three strangers lodged with the simple peasant people in the valley, partaking with thankfulness of the coarse bread, the dates and the red wine—the common fare of their daily life. Nor did they fail to notice a motto inscribed above the fireplace in rude Greek letters:

On the morrow they were ready to begin their search together for the Christ, and they hoped not to wander far before they should find at least the outskirts of His kingdom. But whither should they go? In what direction should they first turn their steps?

Once More a Star

While they were thus wondering and debating, Balthazar suddenly exclaimed: "I see the star!" And behold, a little way before them, and at no great distance above their heads, they discerned in the gray of the early morning a star of pale, opal light, which seemed to move forward as the men moved toward it.

"We must follow the star!" Balthazar said in a whisper. Silently and breathlessly his companions followed on.

Now, so intently did the three men keep their eyes fixed upon the star, and so eagerly did they follow in the direction where it seemed to lead, that it was only after a considerable time they discovered that they had become separated from each other, and that their paths were getting farther and farther apart. Yet, there before each of them was the star, shining with its soft, opalescent light, and still ringing in their ears were the words of Balthazar—"we must follow the star."

The Star Stands Still

So each followed the star, each by himself alone. Gaspard's path wound along near the shore of the gulfs and bays of the Mediterranean, until at last the the star turned southward and drew him nearer and nearer to a great city, and finally stood still over the dome of a vast cathedral. "It must be," thought Gaspard, "that I have come to the end of my search. This must be the capital and palace of the eternal king."

Marbled Aisle's Magnificence

The square in front of the cathedral was thronged with people; multitudes were pouring in through the great portals. Gaspard joined the throngs, and at last found himself under the mighty dome, which seemed to him as far away as the sky itself. Everything in this wonderful place appealed to his imagination. There were great rows of massive columns, symbol of a strength eternal, and they seemed like wide-open arms holding out a welcome to the human race. There were statues and paintings by great masters in art. The light of the sun poured in through many-colored windows, on which were blazoned the deeds of heroes and saints. Strains of music from the great organ in the distance floated out upon the air. Touched and thrilled by all he saw, Gaspard exclaimed to himself: "The place on which I stand is holy ground."

Kyrie Eleison

Soon, however, he perceived that the throngs of people were not lingering, like himself, in awe and wonder over the great columns and the dome, and the statues, and the paintings, and the windows. Their eyes were fixed intently upon something that was going on in the far end of the cathedral. An altar was there, and priests in white robes passing up and down before it, and tall tapers burning around it. Near the altar was the image of a man hanging from a cross; his hands and feet were pierced with nails, and a cruel wound was in his side. The people were gazing at this altar, and at the image, and at what the white-robed priests were doing. The strains of solemn music from the organ blended with the voices of priests chanting the service. Clouds of incense rose from censers, swung with solemn motion by the altar-boys, and the fragrance of the incense was wafted down the long aisles. At last, the tinkling of a bell. The organ became silent for an instant, as though it felt within its heart the awful solemnity of the moment; and then it burst forth into new rapture, and the people began pouring out through the great doors.

We Must Follow the Star

Gaspard went forth with the throng into the cathedral square. "And this," he said, "is the end of my search. I have found the Christ. His kingdom is in the imagination of man. How beautiful, how wonderful, how strange it was! 'Dominus vobiscum,' did not the priests say? Here, then, at last I have found the city of the great King."

But as he lingered, behold! the star which had stood over the dome of the cathedral was now before him, as at first, and seemed to waver and tremble, as if beckoning him on. So, although his feet seemed bound to the spot, and his heart was still throbbing with the deep feelings the cathedral service had created in him, remembering the words of Balthazar, "we must follow the star," he slowly and reluctantly walked on.

The Just Shall Live by Faith

In the meantime Melchoir also had followed faithfully the path along which the star seemed to lead. Through forests in which he almost lost his way, across rivers difficult and dangerous to ford—still he followed on. At length Melchoir's star seemed to tarry over the spire of a gothic church, into which the people were going in throngs. Waiting a moment, to be sure that the star was actually standing still, Melchoir went in with the rest. In this place was no altar, such as Gaspard saw; no image on the cross; no white-robed priests; no swinging censers.

But, as Melchoir entered he heard strains from the organ, and a chorus of voices was singing an anthem beginning with the words, "Te Deum Laudamus." And when the anthem came to a close, a man clothed in a black robe, such as scholars were wont to wear, rose in his place upon a platform elevated above the people, and began to speak to them about the kingdom of Christ. Melchoir listened in eager expectancy. The Truth Shall Make You Free "The kingdom of the Christ," the preacher said, "is the kingdom of the truth, and the truth is to be continued and kept alive by the strength of man's belief. Those things which have been handed down by holy men and sacred oracles since Christ was here upon the earth, are the truths by which we live. How can Christ live except He live in our beliefs? Why did the Father of all intrust us with our reasons, unless it were that we should make them the instruments of our faith and our salvation? Let us therefore stand in our places, while we recite together the articles of our holy faith."

These and many such words did the scholar-preacher declare. And as he sat there with the people, Melchoir felt the weight of the solemn and earnest words, and he said: "So at last have I come to the end of my search. The kingdom of Christ is in the mind of man. His kingdom is the kingdom of the truth."

More Light Shall Break Forth

Then he followed the throngs as they went forth from the church; but the star which had tarried over the lofty spire was now before him, and the opal light wavered and trembled, as if beckoning him on; and the words of the preacher, "we must believe," seemed to blend with the words of Balthazar, "we must follow the star." So, reluctantly and slowly he followed on.

Thy Sacramental Liturgies

But Balthazar—whither went he, following the star? Over many a rugged way, through many a tangled thicket, through valleys and over hills. His star tarried over no cathedrals; it lingered over no Gothic spires. It seemed capricious and restless and tireless. At times it seemed intent on coming to a pause over the head of some human being, but perhaps it was because these human beings themselves were so restless and so busy that the star could not accomplish its intent. For Balthazar saw these men and women hurrying hither and thither on errands of mercy, or deeds of justice; he saw them ferreting out great wrongs, laying heavy blows on the backs of men who oppressed and defrauded their fellow men.

At length Balthazar seemed to understand the movements of the star, and, drawing nearer, he would seem to hear these men repeating cheering and encouraging words to one another. "Pure religion and undefiled," he heard one exclaiming, "is to visit the fatherless and widows in their affliction, and to keep himself unspotted from the world." And another echoed, "Inasmuch as we do it to the least of these, we do it unto Christ."

The Joy of Doing Good

"Ah! thought Balthazar as he listened, I see the meaning of it now; I am coming to the end of my search. The kingdom of Christ—I have found it. It is in the deeds of men; it is in the conscience and the serving will. Devotion to right, this is the law of the kingdom of Christ."

Then Balthazar turned to go in search of his comrades again; but behold! the opal star was trembling, as if beckoning him on. So, still doubting if he had reached the end of his search, he followed the star.

The Paths Converge

Thus Gaspard, Melchoir and Balthazar, each following the star, at last approached each other. The star of each seemed to melt and blend into the star of the others, and the opal light stood at last in the center of the group. Gaspard exclaimed: "I have found that which we all were seeking. The kingdom of Christ is in the imagination; Christ lives in what man feels."

"Nay," said Melchoir, "I have followed the star, and I have found what we sought. The kingdom of Christ is in the reason of man. Christ lives in what man believes."

"But," cried Balthazar, "my star has led me to a different end. The kingdom of Christ is in the will of man. Christ lives in what man does."

"The truth," once more exclaimed Melchoir, "is the law of the kingdom."

"Not truth," declared Balthazar, "but justice, righteousness, goodness and purity—these are its laws and its marks."

"Nay, comrades beloved, hearken to me," answered Gaspard, "it is the miracle of the divine presence. It is God among men, realized in the holy mass. I beheld it all in yonder cathedral."

But lo! once more the star began to tremble and to change its place.

"Let us follow the star!" Balthazar whispered. "We will follow it," echoed the other two.

Once More the Quest

Then the star led them on, and they followed together until they came at length to the doorway of a little cottage; and within the cottage they saw a woman bending over a cradle, and in the cradle a little child lay sleeping. She was a peasant woman; her clothing was not rich; the furnishing of the cottage was humble and scanty. The cradle itself was rude, as if put together by hands unskilful in tasks like that. But when the mother looked at her babe a sweet smile played about her lips, and a light was in her eyes. Then all suddenly the three men remembered another scene long before, when they were bearers of gold and frankincense and myrrh to another babe.

He That Loveth Knoweth God

And while they stood and wondered by the door, there came a strong and sturdy peasant, broad-shouldered, roughly clad, his face browned in the sun, his hands hardened with toil. He came and stood beside the woman, and they bent together over the cradle of the sleeping child, and the man drew the woman tenderly toward him and kissed her brow.

And still the three men lingered; for behold! the star stood still above the child, and they dared not speak. But the heart of Gaspard was saying in silence, "There is something greater than the repeated miracle of the mass."

And Melchoir was thinking, "There is something mightier even than the mind; something superior to naked truth."

For God Is Love

And Balthazar was confessing to himself that he had found something more potent even than the righteous deed. For here they all beheld how life was made sweet and blessed and holy by the power of love; and by love for a little child, in whom was all weakness and helplessness, whose only voice was a cry, but who was all strong and mighty with the power of God, because he could transform roughness into tenderness, and selfishness into loving care, and poverty itself into gifts of gold and fragrant myrrh.

"Truly, my comrades," Balthazar said, "love is the greatest of all."

"And now I understand," said Gaspard, "how the weak things of the world can confound the mighty."

"And I," added Melchoir, "see what it means for God to come to earth in the form of a little child."

And so they turned away, and the radiance of the star was round about them, and they were saying to each other: "Our search at last is ended."

At Christmas Time

By

Anton Chekhov

I

"WHAT shall I write?" asked Yegor, dipping his pen in the ink.

Vasilissa had not seen her daughter for four years. Efimia had gone away to St. Petersburg with her husband after her wedding, had written two letters, and then had vanished as if the earth had engulfed her, not a word nor a sound had come from her since. So now, whether the aged mother was milking the cow at daybreak, or lighting the stove, or dozing at night, the tenor of her thoughts was always the same: "How is Efimia? Is she alive and well?" She wanted to send her a letter, but the old father could not write, and there was no one whom they could ask to write it for them.

But now Christmas had come, and Vasilissa could endure the silence no longer. She went to the tavern to see Yegor, the innkeeper's wife's brother, who had done nothing but sit idly at home in the tavern since he had come back from military service, but of whom people said that he wrote the most beautiful letters, if only one paid him enough. Vasilissa talked with the cook at the tavern, and with the innkeeper's wife, and finally with Yegor himself, and at last they agreed on a price of fifteen copecks.

So now, on the second day of the Christmas festival, Yegor was sitting at a table in the inn kitchen with a pen in his hand. Vasilissa was standing in front of him, plunged in thought, with a look of care and sorrow on her face. Her husband, Peter, a tall, gaunt old man with a bald, brown head, had accompanied her. He was staring steadily in front of him like a blind man; a pan of pork that was frying on the stove was sizzling and puffing, and seeming to say: "Hush, hush, hush!" The kitchen was hot and close.

"What shall I write?" Yegor asked again.

"What's that?" asked Vasilissa, looking at him angrily and suspiciously. "Don't hurry me! You are writing this letter for money, not for love! Now then, begin. To our esteemed son-in-law, Andrei Khrisanfltch, and our only and beloved daughter Efimia, we send greetings and love, and the everlasting blessing of their parents."

"All right, fire away!"

"We wish them a happy Christmas. We are alive and well, and we wish the same for you in the name of God, our Father in heaven--our Father in heaven--"

Vasilissa stopped to think, and exchanged glances with the old man.

"We wish the same for you in the name of God, our Father in Heaven--" she repeated and burst into tears.

That was all she could say. Yet she had thought, as she had lain awake thinking night after night, that ten letters could not contain all she wanted to say. Much water had flowed into the sea since their daughter had gone away with her husband, and the old people had been as lonely as orphans, sighing sadly in the night hours, as if they had buried their child. How many things had happened in the village in all these years! How many people had married, how many had died! How long the winters had been, and how long the nights!

"My, but it's hot!" exclaimed Yegor, unbuttoning his waistcoat. "The temperature must be seventy! Well, what next?" he asked.

The old people answered nothing.

"What is your son-in-law's profession?"

"He used to be a soldier, brother; you know that," replied the old man in a feeble voice. "He went into military service at the same time you did. He used to be a soldier, but now he is in a hospital where a doctor treats sick people with water. He is the door-keeper there."

"You can see it written here," said the old woman, taking a letter out of her handkerchief. "We got this from Efimia a long, long time ago. She may not be alive now."

Yegor reflected a moment, and then began to write swiftly.

"Fate has ordained you for the military profession," he wrote, "therefore we recommend you to look into the articles on disciplinary punishment and penal laws of the war department, and to find there the laws of civilisation for members of that department."

When this was written he read it aloud whilst Vasilissa thought of how she would like to write that there had been a famine last year, and that their flour had not even lasted until Christmas, so that they had been obliged to sell their cow; that the old man was often ill, and must soon surrender his soul to God; that they needed money--but how could she put all this into words? What should she say first and what last?

"Turn your attention to the fifth volume of military definitions," Yegor wrote. "The word soldier is a general appellation, a distinguishing term. Both the commander-in-chief of an army and the last infantryman in the ranks are alike called soldiers--"

The old man's lips moved and he said in a low voice:

"I should like to see my little grandchildren!"

"What grandchildren?" asked the old woman crossly. "Perhaps there are no grandchildren."

"No grandchildren? But perhaps there are! Who knows?"

"And from this you may deduce," Yegor hurried on, "which is an internal, and which is a foreign enemy. Our greatest internal enemy is Bacehus--"

The pen scraped and scratched, and drew long, curly lines like fish-hooks across the paper. Yegor wrote at full speed and underlined each sentence two or three times. He was sitting on a stool with his legs stretched far apart under the table, a fat, lusty creature with a fiery nape and the face of a bulldog. He was the very essence of coarse, arrogant, stiff-necked vulgarity, proud to have been born and bred in a pot-house, and Vasilissa well knew how vulgar he was, but could not find words to express it, and could only glare angrily and suspiciously at him. Her head ached from the sound of his voice and his unintelligible words, and from the oppressive heat of the room, and her mind was confused. She could neither think nor speak, and could only stand and wait for Yegor's pen to stop scratching. But the old man was looking at the writer with unbounded confidence in his eyes. He trusted his old woman who had brought him here, he trusted Yegor, and, when he had spoken of the hydropathic establishment just now, his face had shown that he trusted that, and the healing power of its waters.

When the letter was written, Yegor got up and read it aloud from beginning to end. The old man understood not a word, but he nodded his head confidingly, and said:

"Very good. It runs smoothly. Thank you kindly, it is very good."

They laid three five-copeck pieces on the table and went out. The old man walked away staring straight ahead of him like a blind man, and a look of utmost confidence lay in his eyes, but Vasilissa, as she left the tavern, struck at a dog in her path and exclaimed angrily:

"Ugh--the plague!"

All that night the old woman lay awake full of restless thoughts, and at dawn she rose, said her prayers, and walked eleven miles to the station to post the letter.

II

Doctor Moselweiser's hydropathic establishment was open on New Year's Day as usual; the only difference was that Andrei Khrisaufitch, the doorkeeper, was wearing unusually shiny boots and a uniform trimmed with new gold braid, and that he wished every one who came in a happy New Year.

It was morning. Andrei was standing at the door reading a paper. At ten o'clock precisely an old general came in who was one of the regular visitors of the establishment. Behind him came the postman. Andrei took the general's cloak, and said:

"A happy New Year to your Excellency!"

"Thank you, friend, the same to you!"

And as he mounted the stairs the general nodded toward a closed door and asked, as he did every day, always forgetting the answer:

"And what is there in there?"

"A room for massage, your Excellency."

When the general's footsteps had died away, Andrei looked over the letters and found one addressed to him.

He opened it, read a few lines, and then, still looking at his newspaper, sauntered toward the little room downstairs at the end of a passage where he and his family lived. His wife Efimia was sitting on the bed feeding a baby, her oldest boy was standing at her knee with his curly head in her lap, and a third child was lying asleep on the bed.

Andrei entered their little room, and handed the letter to his wife, saying:

"This must be from the village."

Then he went out again, without raising his eyes from his newspaper, and stopped in the passage not far from the door. He heard Efimia read the first lines in a trembling voice. She could go no farther, but these were enough. Tears streamed from her eyes and she threw her arms round her eldest child and began talking to him and covering him with kisses. It was hard to tell whether she was laughing or crying.

"This is from granny and granddaddy," she cried-- "from the village--oh, Queen of Heaven!-- Oh! holy saints! The roofs are piled with snow there now--and the trees are white, oh, so white! The little children are out coasting on their dear little sleddies--and granddaddy darling, with his dear bald head is sitting by the big, old, warm stove, and the little brown doggie--oh, my precious chickabiddies--"

Andrei remembered as he listened to her that his wife had given him letters at three or four different times, and had asked him to send them to the village, but important business had always interfered, and the letters had remained lying about unposted.

"And the little white hares are skipping about in the fields now--" sobbed Efimia, embracing her boy with streaming eyes. "Granddaddy dear is so kind and good, and granny is so kind and so full of pity. People's hearts are soft and warm in the village-- There is a little church there, and the men sing in the choir. Oh, take us away from here, Queen of Heaven! Intercede for us, merciful mother!"

Andrei returned to his room to smoke until the next patient should come in, and Efimia suddenly grew still and wiped her eyes; only her lips quivered. She was afraid of him, oh, so afraid! She quaked and shuddered at every look and every footstep of his, and never dared to open her mouth in his presence.

Andrei lit a cigarette, but at that moment a bell rang upstairs. He put out his cigarette, and assuming a very solemn expression, hurried to the front door.

The old general, rosy and fresh from his bath, was descending the stairs.

"And what is there in there?" he asked, pointing to a closed door.

Andrei drew himself up at attention, and answered in a loud voice:

"The hot douche, your Excellency."

Little Gretchen and the Wooden Shoe

By

Elizabeth Harrison

Once upon a time, a long time ago, far away across the great ocean, in a country called Germany, there could be seen a small log hut on the edge of a great forest, whose fir trees extended for miles and miles to the north. This little house, made of heavy hewn logs, had but one room in it. A rough pine door gave entrance to this room, and a small square window admitted the light. At the back of the house was built an old-fashioned stone chimney, out of which in winter curled a thin, blue smoke, showing that there was not very much fire within.

Small as the house was, it was large enough for two people who lived in it. I want to tell you a story today about these two people. One was an old gray-haired woman, so old that the little children of the village, nearly half a mile away, often wondered whether she had come into the world with the huge mountains and the giant fir trees, which stood like giants back of her small hut. Her face was wrinkled all over with deep lines, which, if the children could only have read aright, would have told them of many years of cheerful, happy, self-sacrifice; of loving, anxious, watching beside sick-beds; of quiet endurance of pain, of many a day of hunger and cold, and of a thousand deeds of unselfish love for other people; but, of course, they could not read this strange handwriting. They only knew that she was old and wrinkled, and that she stooped as she walked. None of them seemed to fear her, for her smile was always cheerful, and she had a kindly word for each of them if they chanced to meet her on her way to and from the village. With this old, old woman lived a very little girl. So bright and happy was she that the travellers who passed by the lonesome little house on the edge of the forest often thought of a sunbeam as they saw her. These two people were known in the village as Granny Goodyear and Little Gretchen.

The winter had come and the frost had snapped off many of the smaller branches of the pine trees in the forest. Gretchen and her granny were up by daybreak each morning. After their simple breakfast of oatmeal, Gretchen would run to the little closet and fetch Granny's old woolen shawl, which seemed almost as old as Granny herself. Gretchen always claimed the right to put the shawl over Granny's head, even though she had to climb onto the wooden bench to do it. After carefully pinning it under Granny's chin, she gave her a good-bye kiss, and Granny started out for her morning's work in the forest. This work was nothing more nor less than the gathering up of the twigs and branches which autumn winds and winter frosts had thrown upon the ground. These were carefully gathered into a large bundle which Granny tied together with a strong linen band. She then managed to lift the bundle to her shoulder and trudged off to the village with it. Here she sold the fagots for kindling wood to the people of the village. Sometimes she would get only a few pence each day, and sometimes a dozen or more, but on this money little Gretchen and she managed to live; they had their home, and the forest kindly furnished the wood for the fire which kept them warm in winter.

In the summer time Granny had a little garden at the back of the house, where she raised, with little Gretchen's help, a few potatoes and turnips and onions. These she carefully stored away for winter use. To this meagre supply, the pennies, gained by selling the twigs from the forest, added the oatmeal for Gretchen and a little black coffee for Granny. Meat was a thing they never thought of having. It cost too much money. Still, Granny and Gretchen were very happy, because they loved each other dearly. Sometimes Gretchen would be left alone all day long in the hut, because Granny would have some work to do in the village after selling her bundle of sticks and twigs. It was during these long days that little Gretchen had taught herself to sing the song which the wind sang to the pine branches. In the summer time she learned the chirp and twitter of the birds, until her voice might almost be mistaken for a bird's voice, she learned to dance as the swaying shadows did, and even to talk to the stars which shone through the little square window when Granny came home late or too tired to talk.

Sometimes, when the weather was fine, or her Granny had an extra bundle of knitted stockings to take to the village, she would let little Gretchen go along with her. It chanced that one of these trips to the town came just the week before Christmas, and Gretchen's eyes were delighted by the sight of the lovely Christmas trees which stood in the window of the village store. It seemed to her that she would never tire of looking at the knit dolls, the woolly lambs, the little wooden shops with their queer, painted men and women in them, and all the other fine things. She had never owned a plaything in her whole life; therefore, toys which you and I would not think much of seemed to her very beautiful.

That night, after their supper of baked potatoes was over, and little Gretchen had cleared away the dishes and swept up the hearth, because Granny dear was so tired, she brought her own little wooden stool and placed it very near Granny's feet and sat down upon it, folding her hands on her lap. Granny knew that this meant that she wanted to be told about something, so she smilingly laid away the large Bible which she had been reading, and took up her knitting, which was as much as to say: "Well, Gretchen, dear, Granny is ready to listen."

"Granny," said Gretchen slowly, "It's almost Christmas time, isn't it?"

"Yes, dearie," said Granny, "only five days more now," and then she sighed, but little Gretchen was so happy that she did not notice Granny's sigh.

"What do you think, Granny, I'll get this Christmas?" said she, looking up eagerly into Granny's face.

"Ah, child, child," said Granny, shaking her head, "you'll have no Christmas this year. We are too poor for that."

"Oh, but Granny," interrupted little Gretchen, "think of all the beautiful toys we saw in the village today. Surely Santa Claus has sent enough for every little child."

"Ah, dearie, those toys are for people who can pay for them, and we have no money to spend for Christmas toys."

"Well, Granny," said Gretchen, "perhaps some of the little children who live in the great house on the hill at the other end of the village, will be willing to share some of their toys with me. They will be glad to give some to a little girl who has none."

"Dear child, dear child," said Granny, leaning forward and stroking the soft, shiny hair of the little girl, "your heart is full of love. You would be glad to bring a Christmas to every child; but their heads are so full of what they are going to get that they forget all about anybody else but themselves." Then she sighed and shook her head.

"Well, Granny," said Gretchen, her bright, happy tone of voice growing a little less joyous, "perhaps the dear Santa Claus will show some of the village children how to make presents that do not cost money, and some of them may surprise me Christmas morning with a present. And, Granny, dear," added she, springing up from her low stool, "can't I gather some of the pine branches and take them to the old sick man who lives in the house by the mill, so that he can have the sweet smell of our forest in his room all Christmas day?"

"Yes, dearie," said Granny, "you may do what you can to make the Christmas bright and happy, but you must not expect any present yourself."

"Oh, but, Granny," said little Gretchen, her face brightening, "you forgot all about the shining Christmas angels, who came down to earth and sang their wonderful song the night the beautiful Christ-Child was born! They are so loving and good that *they* will not forget any little child. I shall ask my dear stars tonight to tell them of us. You know," she added, with a look of relief, "the stars are so very high that they must know the angels quite well as they come and go with their messages from the loving God."

Granny sighed as she half whispered. "Poor child, poor child!" but Gretchen threw her arm around Granny's neck and gave her a hearty kiss, saying as she did so: "Oh, Granny, Granny, you don't talk to the stars often enough, else you would not be sad at Christmas time." Then she danced all around the room, whirling her little skirts about her to show Granny how the wind had made the snow dance that day. She looked so droll and funny that Granny forgot her cares and worries and laughed with little Gretchen over her new snow dance. The days passed on and the morning before Christmas Eve came. Gretchen having tidied up the little room—for Granny had taught her to be a careful little housewife—was off to the forest, singing a birdlike song, almost as happy and free as the birds themselves. She was very busy that day preparing a surprise for Granny. First, however, she gathered the most beautiful of the fir branches within her reach to take the next morning to the old sick man who lived by the mill.

The day was all too short for the happy little girl. When Granny came trudging wearily home that night, she found the frame of the doorway covered with green pine branches.

"It is to welcome you, Granny! It is to welcome you!" cried Gretchen; "our dear old home wanted to give you a Christmas welcome. Don't you see, the branches of the evergreen make it look as if it were smiling all over, and it is trying to say, 'A happy Christmas to you Granny'."

Granny laughed and kissed the little girl, as they opened the door and went in together. Here was a new surprise for Granny. The four posts of the wooden bed, which stood in one corner of the room, had been trimmed by the busy little fingers, with smaller and more flexible branches of the pine trees. A small bouquet of red mountain ash berries stood at each side of the fireplace, and these, together with the trimmed posts of the bed, gave the plain old room quite a festive look. Gretchen laughed and clapped her hands and danced about until the house seemed full of music to poor, tired Granny, whose heart had been sad as she turned toward their home that night, thinking of the disappointment that must come to loving little Gretchen the next morning.

After supper was over little Gretchen drew her stool up to Granny's side, and laying her soft, little hands on Granny's knee asked to be told once again the story of the coming of the Christ-Child; how the night that he was born the beautiful angels had sung their wonderful song, and how the whole sky had become bright with a strange and glorious light, never seen by the people of earth before. Gretchen had heard the story many, many times before, but she never grew tired of it, and now that Christmas Eve had come again, the happy little child wanted to hear it once more.

When Granny had finished telling it the two sat quiet and silent for a little while thinking it over; then Granny rose and said that it was time for her to go to bed. She slowly took off her heavy wooden shoes, such as are worn in that country, and placed them beside the hearth. Gretchen looked thoughtfully at them for a minute or two, and then she said, "Granny, don't you think that *somebody* in all this wide world will think of us tonight?"

"Nay, Gretchen, I do not think any one will."

"Well, then, Granny," said Gretchen, "the Christmas angels will, I know; so I am going to take one of your wooden shoes and put it on the windowsill outside, so that they may see it as they pass by. I am sure the stars will tell the Christmas angels where the shoe is."

"Ah, you foolish, foolish child," said Granny, "you are only getting ready for a disappointment. Tomorrow morning there will be nothing whatever in the shoe. I can tell you that now."

But little Gretchen would not listen. She only shook her head and cried out: "Ah, Granny, you do not talk enough to the stars." With this she seized the shoe, and opening the door, hurried out to place it on the window sill. It was very dark without and something soft and cold seemed to gently kiss her hair and face. Gretchen knew by this that it was snowing, and she looked up to the sky, anxious to see if the stars were in sight, but a strong wind was tumbling the dark, heavy snow-clouds about and had shut away all else.

"Never mind," said Gretchen softly to herself, "the stars are up there, even if I can't see them, and the Christmas angels do not mind snow storms."

Just then a rough wind went sweeping by the little girl, whispering something to her which she could not understand, and then it made a sudden rush up to the snow clouds and parted them, so that the deep mysterious sky appeared beyond, and shining down out of the midst of it was Gretchen's favorite star.

"Ah, little star, little star!" said the child, laughing aloud, "I knew you were there, though I could not see you. Will you whisper to the Christmas angels as they come by that little Gretchen wants so very much to have a Christmas gift tomorrow morning, if they have one to spare, and that she has put one of Granny's shoes upon the windowsill for it?"

A moment more and the little girl, standing on tiptoe had reached the windowsill and placed the shoe upon it, and was back again in the house beside Granny and the warm fire.

The two went quietly to bed, and that night as little Gretchen knelt to pray to the Heavenly Father, she thanked him for having sent the Christ-Child into the world to teach all mankind to be loving and unselfish, and in a few minutes she was sleeping, dreaming of the Christmas angels.

The next morning, very early, even before the sun was up, little Gretchen was awakened by the sound of sweet music coming from the village. She listened for a moment and then she knew that the choir boys were singing the Christmas carols in the open air of the village street. She sprang up out of bed and began to dress herself as quickly as possible, singing as she dressed. While Granny was slowly putting on her clothes, little

Gretchen having finished dressing herself, unfastened the door and hurried out to see what the Christmas angels had left in the old wooden shoe.

The white snow covered everything—trees, stumps, roads, and pastures—until the whole world looked like fairy land. Gretchen climbed up on a large stone which was beneath the window and carefully lifted down the wooden shoe. The snow tumbled off of it in a shower over the little girl's hands, but she did not heed that; she ran hurriedly back into the house, putting her hand into the toe of the shoe as she ran.

"Oh, Granny, Granny!" she exclaimed; "you did not believe the Christmas angels would think about us, but see, they have, they have! Here is a dear little bird nestled down in the toe of your shoe! Oh, isn't he beautiful?"

Granny came forward and looked at what the child was holding lovingly in her hand. There she saw a tiny chick-a-dee, whose wing was evidently broken by the rough and boisterous winds of the night before, and who had taken shelter in the safe, dry toe of the old wooden shoe. She gently took the little bird out of Gretchen's hands, and skilfully bound his broken wing to his side, so that he need not hurt himself trying to fly with it. Then she showed Gretchen how to make a nice warm nest for the little stranger, close beside the fire and when their breakfast was ready, she let Gretchen feed the little bird with a few moist crumbs.

Later in the day Gretchen carried the fresh, green boughs to the old sick man by the mill, and on her way home stopped to enjoy the Christmas toys of some other children that she knew, never once wishing they were hers. When she reached home she found that the little bird had gone to sleep. Soon, however, he opened his eyes and stretched his head up, saying just as plain as a bird can say:

"Now, my new friends, I want you to give me something more to eat." Gretchen gladly fed him again, and then, holding him in her lap, she softly and gently stroked his gray feathers until the little creature seemed to lose all fear of her. That evening Granny taught her a Christmas hymn and told her another beautiful Christmas story. Then Gretchen made up a funny little story to tell the birdie. He winked his eyes and turned his head from side to side in such a droll fashion that Gretchen laughed until the tears came.

As Granny and she got ready for bed that night, Gretchen put her arms softly around Granny's neck, and whispered: "What a beautiful Christmas we have had today, Granny. Is there anything more lovely in all the world than Christmas?"

"Nay, child, nay," said Granny, "not to such loving hearts as yours."

The Steadfast Tin Soldier

By

Hans Christian Andersen

There were once five-and-twenty tin soldiers. They were all brothers, born of the same old tin spoon. They shouldered their muskets and looked straight ahead of them, splendid in their uniforms, all red and blue.

The very first thing in the world that they heard was, "Tin soldiers!" A small boy shouted it and clapped his hands as the lid was lifted off their box on his birthday. He immediately set them up on the table.

All the soldiers looked exactly alike except one. He looked a little different as he had been cast last of all. The tin was short, so he had only one leg. But there he stood, as steady on one leg as any of the other soldiers on their two. But just you see, he'll be the remarkable one.

On the table with the soldiers were many other playthings, and one that no eye could miss was a marvelous castle of cardboard. It had little windows through which you could look right inside it. And in front of the castle were miniature trees around a little mirror supposed to represent a lake. The wax swans that swam on its surface were reflected in the mirror. All this was very pretty but prettiest of all was the little lady who stood in the open doorway of the castle. Though she was a paper doll, she wore a dress of the fluffiest gauze. A tiny blue ribbon went over her shoulder for a scarf, and in the middle of it shone a spangle that was as big as her face. The little lady held out both her arms, as a ballet dancer does, and one leg was lifted so high behind her that the tin soldier couldn't see it at all, and he supposed she must have only one leg, as he did.

"That would be a wife for me," he thought. "But maybe she's too grand. She lives in a castle. I have only a box, with four-and-twenty roommates to share it. That's no place for her. But I must try to make her acquaintance." Still as stiff as when he stood at attention, he lay down on the table behind a snuffbox, where he could admire the dainty little dancer who kept standing on one leg without ever losing her balance.

When the evening came the other tin soldiers were put away in their box, and the people of the house went to bed. Now the toys began to play among themselves at visits, and battles, and at giving balls. The tin soldiers rattled about in their box, for they wanted to play too, but they could not get the lid open. The nutcracker turned somersaults, and the slate pencil squeaked out jokes on the slate. The toys made such a noise that they woke up the canary bird, who made them a speech, all in verse. The only two who stayed still were the tin soldier and the little dancer. Without ever swerving from the tip of one toe, she held out her arms to him, and the tin soldier was just as steadfast on his one leg. Not once did he take his eyes off her.

Then the clock struck twelve and - clack! - up popped the lid of the snuffbox. But there was no snuff in it, no- out bounced a little black bogey, a jack-in-the-box.

"Tin soldier," he said. "Will you please keep your eyes to yourself?" The tin soldier pretended not to hear.

The bogey said, "Just you wait till tomorrow."

But when morning came, and the children got up, the soldier was set on the window ledge. And whether the bogey did it, or there was a gust of wind, all of a sudden the window flew open and the soldier pitched out headlong from the third floor. He fell at breathtaking speed and landed cap first, with his bayonet buried between the paving stones and his one leg stuck straight in the air. The housemaid and the little boy ran down to look for him and, though they nearly stepped on the tin soldier, they walked right past without seeing him. If the soldier had called, "Here I am!" they would surely have found him, but he thought it contemptible to raise an uproar while he was wearing his uniform.

Soon it began to rain. The drops fell faster and faster, until they came down by the bucketful. As soon as the rain let up, along came two young rapscallions.

"Hi, look!" one of them said, "there's a tin soldier. Let's send him sailing."

They made a boat out of newspaper, put the tin soldier in the middle of it, and away he went down the gutter with the two young rapscallions running beside him and clapping their hands. High heavens! How the waves splashed, and how fast the water ran down the gutter. Don't forget that it had just been raining by the bucketful. The paper boat pitched, and tossed, and sometimes it whirled about so rapidly that it made the soldier's head spin. But he stood as steady as ever. Never once flinching, he kept his eyes front, and carried his gun shoulder-high. Suddenly the boat rushed under a long plank where the gutter was boarded over. It was as dark as the soldier's own box.

"Where can I be going?" the soldier wondered. "This must be that black bogey's revenge. Ah! if only I had the little lady with me, it could be twice as dark here for all that I would care."

Out popped a great water rat who lived under the gutter plank.

"Have you a passport?" said the rat. "Hand it over."

The soldier kept quiet and held his musket tighter. On rushed the boat, and the rat came right after it, gnashing his teeth as he called to the sticks and straws:

"Halt him! Stop him! He didn't pay his toll. He hasn't shown his passport. "But the current ran stronger and stronger. The soldier could see daylight ahead where the board ended, but he also heard a roar that would frighten the bravest of us. Hold on! Right at the end of that gutter plank the water poured into the great canal. It was as dangerous to him as a waterfall would be to us.

He was so near it he could not possibly stop. The boat plunged into the whirlpool. The poor tin soldier stood as staunch as he could, and no one can say that he so much as blinked an eye. Thrice and again the boat spun around. It filled to the top - and was bound to sink. The water was up to his neck and still the boat went down, deeper, deeper, deeper, and the paper got soft and limp. Then the water rushed over his head. He thought of the pretty little dancer whom he'd never see again, and in his ears rang an old, old song:

"Farewell, farewell, O warrior brave,

Nobody can from Death thee save."

And now the paper boat broke beneath him, and the soldier sank right through. And just at that moment he was swallowed by a most enormous fish.

My! how dark it was inside that fish. It was darker than under the gutter-plank and it was so cramped, but the tin soldier still was staunch. He lay there full length, soldier fashion, with musket to shoulder.

Then the fish flopped and floundered in a most unaccountable way. Finally it was perfectly still, and after a while something struck through him like a flash of lightning. The tin soldier saw daylight again, and he heard a voice say, "The Tin Soldier!" The fish had been caught, carried to market, bought, and brought to a kitchen where the cook cut him open with her big knife.

She picked the soldier up bodily between her two fingers, and carried him off upstairs. Everyone wanted to see this remarkable traveler who had traveled about in a fish's stomach, but the tin soldier took no pride in it. They put him on the table and-lo and behold, what curious things can happen in this world-there he was, back in the same room as before. He saw the same children, the same toys were on the table, and there was the same fine castle with the pretty little dancer. She still balanced on one leg, with the other raised high. She too was steadfast. That touched the soldier so deeply that he would have cried tin tears, only soldiers never cry. He looked at her, and she looked at him, and never a word was said. Just as things were going so nicely for them, one of the little boys snatched up the tin soldier and threw him into the stove. He did it for no reason at all. That black bogey in the snuffbox must have put him up to it.

The tin soldier stood there dressed in flames. He felt a terrible heat, but whether it came from the flames or from his love he didn't know. He'd lost his splendid colors, maybe from his hard journey, maybe from grief, nobody can say.

He looked at the little lady, and she looked at him, and he felt himself melting. But still he stood steadfast, with his musket held trim on his shoulder.

Then the door blew open. A puff of wind struck the dancer. She flew like a sylph, straight into the fire with the soldier, blazed up in a flash, and was gone. The tin soldier melted, all in a lump. The next day, when a servant took up the ashes she found him in the shape of a little tin heart. But of the pretty dancer nothing was left except her spangle, and it was burned as black as a coal.

The Christmas Cuckoo

By

Frances Browne

Once upon a time there stood in the midst of a bleak moor, in the North Country, a certain village. All its inhabitants were poor, for their fields were barren, and they had little trade; but the poorest of them all were two brothers called Scrub and Spare, who followed the cobbler's craft. Their hut was built of clay and wattles. The door was low and always open, for there was no window. The roof did not entirely keep out the rain and the only thing comfortable was a wide fireplace, for which the brothers could never find wood enough to make sufficient fire. There they worked in most brotherly friendship, though with little encouragement.

On one unlucky day a new cobbler arrived in the village. He had lived in the capital city of the kingdom and, by his own account, cobbled for the queen and the princesses. His awls were sharp, his lasts were new; he set up his stall in a neat cottage with two windows. The villagers soon found out that one patch of his would outwear two of the brothers'. In short, all the mending left Scrub and Spare, and went to the new cobbler.

The season had been wet and cold, their barley did not ripen well, and the cabbages never half- closed in the garden. So the brothers were poor that winter, and when Christmas came they had nothing to feast on but a barley loaf and a piece of rusty bacon. Worse than that, the snow was very deep and they could get no firewood.

Their hut stood at the end of the village; beyond it spread the bleak moor, now all white and silent. But that moor had once been a forest; great roots of old trees were still to be found in it, loosened from the soil and laid bare by the winds and rains. One of these, a rough, gnarled log, lay hard by their door, the half of it above the snow, and Spare said to his brother: --

"Shall we sit here cold on Christmas while the great root lies yonder? Let us chop it up for firewood, the work will make us warm."

"No," said Scrub, "it's not right to chop wood on Christmas; besides, that root is too hard to be broken with any hatchet."

"Hard or not, we must have a fire," replied Spare. "Come, brother, help me in with it. Poor as we are there is nobody in the village will have such a yule log as ours."

Scrub liked a little grandeur, and, in hopes of having a fine yule log, both brothers strained and strove with all their might till, between pulling and pushing, the great old root was safe on the hearth, and beginning to crackle and blaze with the red embers.

In high glee the cobblers sat down to their bread and bacon. The door was shut, for there was nothing but cold moonlight and snow outside; but the hut, strewn with fir boughs and ornamented with holly, looked cheerful as the ruddy blaze flared up and rejoiced their hearts.

Then suddenly from out the blazing root they heard: "Cuckoo! cuckoo!" as plain as ever the spring-bird's voice came over the moor on a May morning.

"What is that?" said Scrub, terribly frightened; "it is something bad!"

"Maybe not," said Spare.

And out of the deep hole at the side of the root, which the fire had not reached, flew a large, gray cuckoo, and lit on the table before them. Much as the cobblers had been surprised, they were still more so when it said: --

"Good gentlemen, what season is this?"

"It's Christmas," said Spare.

"Then a merry Christmas to you!" said the cuckoo. "I went to sleep in the hollow of that old root one evening last summer, and never woke till the heat of your fire made me think it was summer again. But now since you have burned my lodging, let me stay in your hut till the spring comes round, -- I only want a hole to sleep in, and when I go on my travels next summer be assured I will bring you some present for your trouble."

"Stay and welcome," said Spare, while Scrub sat wondering if it were something bad or not.

"I'll make you a good warm hole in the thatch," said Spare. "But you must be hungry after that long sleep, -- here is a slice of barley bread. Come help us to keep Christmas!"

The cuckoo ate up the slice, drank water from a brown jug, and flew into a snug hole which Spare scooped for it in the thatch of the hut.

Scrub said he was afraid it would n't be lucky; but as it slept on and the days passed he forgot his fears.

So the snow melted, the heavy rains came, the cold grew less, the days lengthened, and one sunny morning the brothers were awakened by the cuckoo shouting its own cry to let them know the spring had come.

"Now I'm going on my travels," said the bird, "over the world to tell men of the spring. There is no country where trees bud, or flowers bloom, that I will not cry in before the year goes round. Give me another slice of barley bread to help me on my journey, and tell me what present I shall bring you at the twelvemonth's end."

Scrub would have been angry with his brother for cutting so large a slice, their store of barley being low, but his mind was occupied with what present it would be most prudent to ask for.

"There are two trees hard by the well that lies at the world's end," said the cuckoo; "one of them is called the golden tree, for its leaves are all of beaten gold. Every winter they fall into the well with a sound like scattered coin, and I know not what becomes of them. As for the other, it is always green like a laurel. Some call it the wise, and some the merry, tree. Its leaves never fall, but they that get one of them keep a blithe heart in spite of all misfortunes, and can make themselves as merry in a hut as in a palace."

"Good master cuckoo, bring me a leaf off that tree!" cried Spare.

"Now, brother, don't be a fool!" said Scrub; "think of the leaves of beaten gold! Dear master cuckoo, bring me one of them!"

Before another word could be spoken the cuckoo had flown out of the open door, and was shouting its spring cry over moor and meadow.

The brothers were poorer than ever that year. Nobody would send them a single shoe to mend, and Scrub and Spare would have left the village but for their barley-field and their cabbage- garden. They sowed their barley, planted their cabbage, and, now that their trade was gone, worked in the rich villagers' fields to make out a scanty living.

So the seasons came and passed; spring, summer, harvest, and winter followed each other as they have done from the beginning. At the end of the latter Scrub and Spare had grown so poor and ragged that their old neighbors forgot to invite them to wedding feasts or merrymakings, and the brothers thought the cuckoo had forgotten them, too, when at daybreak on the first of April they heard a hard beak knocking at their door, and a voice crying: --

"Cuckoo! cuckoo! Let me in with my presents!"

Spare ran to open the door, and in came the cuckoo, carrying on one side of its bill a golden leaf larger than that of any tree in the North Country; and in the other side of its bill, one like that of the common laurel, only it had a fresher green.

"Here," it said, giving the gold to Scrub and the green to Spare, "it is a long carriage from the world's end. Give me a slice of barley bread, for I must tell the North Country that the spring has come."

Scrub did not grudge the thickness of that slice, though it was cut from their last loaf. So much gold had never been in the cobbler's hands before, and he could not help exulting over his brother.

"See the wisdom of my choice," he said, holding up the large leaf of gold. "As for yours, as good might be plucked from any hedge, I wonder a sensible bird would carry the like so far."

"Good master cobbler," cried the cuckoo, finishing its slice, "your conclusions are more hasty than courteous. If your brother is disappointed this time, I go on the same journey every year, and for your hospitable entertainment will think it no trouble to bring each of you whichever leaf you desire."

"Darling cuckoo," cried Scrub, "bring me a golden one."

And Spare, looking up from the green leaf on which he gazed as though it were a crown-jewel, said: --

"Be sure to bring me one from the merry tree."

And away flew the cuckoo.

"This is the feast of All Fools, and it ought to be your birthday," said Scrub. "Did ever man fling away such an opportunity of getting rich? Much good your merry leaves will do in the midst of rags and poverty!"

But Spare laughed at him, and answered with quaint old proverbs concerning the cares that come with gold, till Scrub, at length getting angry, vowed his brother was not fit to live with a respectable man; and taking his lasts, his awls, and his golden leaf, he left the wattle hut, and went to tell the villagers.

They were astonished at the folly of Spare, and charmed with Scrub's good sense, particularly when he showed them the golden leaf, and told that the cuckoo would bring him one every spring.

The new cobbler immediately took him into partnership; the greatest people sent him their shoes to mend. Fairfeather, a beautiful village maiden, smiled graciously upon him; and in the course of that summer they were married, with a grand wedding feast, at which the whole village danced except Spare, who was not invited, because the bride could not bear his low-mindedness, and his brother thought him a disgrace to the family.

As for Scrub he established himself with Fairfeather in a cottage close by that of the new cobbler, and quite as fine. There he mended shoes to everybody's satisfaction, had a scarlet coat and a fat goose for dinner on holidays. Fairfeather, too, had a crimson gown, and fine blue ribbons; but neither she nor Scrub was content, for to buy this grandeur the golden leaf had to be broken and parted With piece by piece, so the last morsel was gone before the cuckoo came with another.

Spare lived on in the old hut, and worked in the cabbage-garden. [Scrub had got the barley-field because he was the elder.] Every day his coat grew more ragged, and the hut more weather- beaten; but people remarked that he never looked sad or sour. And the wonder was that, from the time any one began to keep his company, he or she grew kinder, happier, and content.

Every first of April the cuckoo came tapping at their doors with the golden leaf for Scrub, and the green for Spare. Fairfeather would have entertained it nobly with wheaten bread and honey, for she had some notion of persuading it to bring two golden leaves instead of one; but the cuckoo flew away to eat barley bread with Spare, saying it was not fit company for fine people, and liked the old hut where it slept so snugly from Christmas till spring.

Scrub spent the golden leaves, and remained always discontented; and Spare kept the merry ones.

I do not know how many years passed in this manner, when a certain great lord, who owned that village, came to the neighborhood. His castle stood on the moor. It was ancient and strong, with high towers and a deep moat. All the country as far as one could see from the highest turret belonged to its lord; but he had not been there for twenty years, and would not have come then only he was melancholy. And there he lived in a very bad temper. The servants said nothing would please him, and the villagers put on their worst clothes lest he should raise their rents.

But one day in the harvest-time His Lordship chanced to meet Spare gathering water-cresses at a meadow stream, and fell into talk with the cobbler. How it was nobody could tell, but from that hour the great lord cast away his melancholy. He forgot all his woes, and went about with a noble train, hunting, fishing, and making merry in his hall, where all travelers were entertained, and all the poor were welcome.

This strange story spread through the North Country, and great company came to the cobbler's hut, -- rich men who had lost their money, poor men who had lost their friends, beauties who had grown old, wits who had gone out of fashion, -- all came to talk with Spare, and, whatever their troubles had been, all went home merry.

The rich gave him presents, the poor gave him thanks. Spare's coat ceased to be ragged, he had bacon with his cabbage, and the villagers began to think there was some sense in him.

By this time his fame had reached the capital city, and even the court. There were a great many discontented people there; and the king had lately fallen into ill humor because a neighboring princess, with seven islands for her dowry, would not marry his eldest son.

So a royal messenger was sent to Spare, with a velvet mantle, a diamond ring, and a command that he should repair to court immediately.

"To-morrow is the first of April," said Spare, "and I will go with you two hours after sunrise."

The messenger lodged all night at the castle, and the cuckoo came at sunrise with the merry leaf.

"Court is a fine place," it said, when the cobbler told it he was going, "but I cannot come there; they would lay snares and catch me; so be careful of the leaves I have brought you, and give me a farewell slice of barley bread."

Spare was sorry to part with the cuckoo, little as he had of its company, but he gave it a slice which would have broken Scrub's heart in former times, it was so thick and large. And having sewed up the leaves in the lining of his leather doublet, he set out with the messenger on his way to court.

His coming caused great surprise there. Everybody wondered what the king could see in such a common-looking man; but scarcely had His Majesty conversed with him half an hour, when the princess and her seven islands were forgotten and orders given that a feast for all comers should be spread in the banquet hall.

The princes of the blood, the great lords and ladies, the ministers of state, after that discoursed with Spare, and the more they talked the lighter grew their hearts, so that such changes had never been seen at court.

The lords forgot their spites and the ladies their envies, the princes and ministers made friends among themselves, and the judges showed no favor.

As for Spare, he had a chamber assigned him in the palace, and a seat at the king's table. One sent him rich robes, and another costly jewels; but in the midst of all his grandeur he still wore the leathern doublet, and continued to live at the king's court, happy and honored, and making all others merry and content.

Little Jean

A Christmas Story

By

François Coppée

Long ago, and far from here, in a country with a name too hard to pronounce, there lived a little boy named Jean. In many ways, he was just like the boys here, for there are many Johns over here, are there not? Then too, Jean lived with his auntie, and some of our boys do that too. His father and mother were dead, and that is true here sometimes, isn't it? But in some ways things were quite different with Jean. In the first place his auntie was very, very cross, and she often made him climb up his ladder to his little garret room to go to sleep on his pallet of straw, without any supper, save a dry crust. His stockings had holes in the heels, and toes and knees, because his auntie never had time to mend them, and his shoes would have been worn out all the time if they had not been such strong wooden shoes—for in that country the boys all wore wooden shoes. Jean did many a little service around the place, for his auntie made him work for his daily bread, and he chopped the wood and swept the paths and made the fires and ran the errands, but he never heard anyone say "Thank you."

Jean's happiest days were at school, and I wonder if he was like our boys in that? There his playmates wore much better clothes and good stockings too, and warm top coats, but they never thought of making fun of Jean, for they all loved to play with him. One morning Jean started off to school (which was next to the big church), and when he got there he found the children all so happy and gay and dressed in their best clothes, and he heard one boy say, "Won't it be jolly tomorrow with the big tree full of oranges and popcorn and candy, and the candles burning?" And another added, "Won't it be fun to see the things in our shoes in the morning, the goodies that boys love?" And another said, "My, but we have a big, fat goose at our house, stuffed with plums and just brown to a turn," and he smacked his lips as he thought of it. And Jean began to wonder about that beautiful tree and wish that one would grow at his house. And he thought about his wooden shoes and knew there would be no goodies in them for him in the morning. Then he heard one boy say, "Don't you love Christmas?" And Jean said, "Christmas! why, what is Christmas?" But just then the teacher came in and said, "Boys, come into the church now and hear the music." And so the boys marched one behind the other just as they do in school here, and they went into the great church. Jean thought it was beautiful in there! The soft light, the warm pleasant air, the flowers, and the marble altar, and then the music! Oh, such music Jean had never heard, and somehow as he sat on the high-backed bench and listened, his own heart grew very warm although he could not understand why, and he loved so to hear them singing: "Peace on earth, good will to men." And it began to sing itself over and over in his heart, this sweet, sweet song of "Peace on earth, good will to men." Then the time came to go home, and the boys all shouted, "Good-bye, Jean! and Merry Christmas!" And though Jean didn't know about "Merry Christmas," he kept singing in his little warmed heart, "Peace on earth, good will to men," and then he was glad the other boys could have the tree and the goose and the wooden shoes full of goodies even if he couldn't.

As Jean went home the snow began to fall and the big flakes lodged on his shoulders and cap and hands, but he didn't mind the cold for his heart was so warm. By and by as he ran down the street he passed a tall house with the steps going up from the street, and there sitting on the bottom step he saw a little boy with soft curling hair and a beautiful face, leaning his head against the stone house, fast asleep. Somehow as Jean looked at the sleeping face, his own heart grew still and quiet and warm, and he felt like he could look at it forever, and suddenly he caught himself singing softly under his breath, "Peace on earth, good will to men." And then he looked down at the little boy's feet and he saw that he was barefooted and his little feet were purple with the cold. As Jean looked at the feet, and then at the face of the child, and thought of the sweet song in his heart, he said, "Oh! I wish I could give him my shoes, for I have stockings to keep me warm, but auntie would be so mad! And the more he looked and thought, the more he longed to give his shoes away, until all at once he said, "I know what I'll do, I'll give him one shoe and one stocking and then he won't be so cold," and he felt as though he couldn't get his shoe and stocking off fast enough to give them to the little child. So gently and tenderly he lifted the little cold foot in his hand to put on the shoe that he did not waken the sleeping boy, even when he had put the stocking on the other foot, and then as he stood up again and took a last look at the lovely face, before he knew it he was singing aloud, "Peace on earth, good will to men." Then he hopped off home in the snow with the happiest heart he had ever had.

Now, I wish the story turned out differently and that his auntie said when he told her about it, "I'm so glad you did it, Jean." But she was so very cross, that she slapped Jean and sent him off to bed without any supper, saying, "You had no right to give away that shoe and stocking for my money paid for them!" Somehow Jean didn't mind doing without supper that night and he soon went fast asleep and dreamed a beautiful dream, for he thought he was still singing "Peace on earth, good will to men!" And he saw a vision of the little sleeping boy, that grew into a tall and gentle man with a radiant face who walked to and fro in Jean's dream, singing with him "Peace on earth, good will to men!" Then morning came and outside his window, Jean heard the voices of children singing, "Glory to God in the highest, on earth peace, good will to men!" And he heard a very strange sound too, for his auntie's voice, soft and gentle, said, "Jean, wake up, and come down and see what has happened," and Jean came down the ladder and lo! there was a wonderful tree just like the other boys were having today, and a goose, and by the fireplace his own wooden shoe, and beside it the mate that he had given to the sleeping child, and far in the distance Jean heard the children's voices singing as they ran down the street, "Peace, peace on earth, good will to men!" Then the room grew very still and peaceful and Jean's heart did too—and through the silence there came a voice so tender and loving—so gentle that the auntie's eyes were full of tears, and Jean wanted to listen forever, and the voice said, "Jean, inasmuch as ye did it unto one of the least of these, my brethren, ye did it unto ME."

The Other Wise Man

By

Henry Van Dyke

You know the story of the Three Wise Men of the East, and how they travelled from far away to offer their gifts at the manger-cradle in Bethlehem. But have you ever heard the story of the Other Wise Man, who also saw the star in its rising, and set out to follow it, yet did not arrive with his brethren in the presence of the young child Jesus? Of the great desire of this fourth pilgrim, and how it was denied, yet accomplished in the denial; of his many wanderings and the probations of his soul; of the long way of his seeking and the strange way of his finding the One whom he sought--I would tell the tale as I have heard fragments of it in the Hall of Dreams, in the palace of the Heart of Man.

I

In the days when Augustus Caesar was master of many kings and Herod reigned in Jerusalem, there lived in the city of Ecbatana, among the mountains of Persia, a certain man named Artaban. His house stood close to the outermost of the walls which encircled the royal treasury. From his roof he could look over the seven-fold battlements of black and white and crimson and blue and red and silver and gold, to the hill where the summer palace of the Parthian emperors glittered like a jewel in a crown.

Around the dwelling of Artaban spread a fair garden, a tangle of flowers and fruit-trees, watered by a score of streams descending from the slopes of Mount Orontes, and made musical by innumerable birds. But all colour was lost in the soft and odorous darkness of the late September night, and all sounds were hushed in the deep charm of its silence, save the plashing of the water, like a voice half-sobbing and half-laughing under the shadows. High above the trees a dim glow of light shone through the curtained arches of the upper chamber, where the master of the house was holding council with his friends.

He stood by the doorway to greet his guests--a tall, dark man of about forty years, with brilliant eyes set near together under his broad brow, and firm lines graven around his fine, thin lips; the brow of a dreamer and the mouth of a soldier, a man of sensitive feeling but inflexible will--one of those who, in whatever age they may live, are born for inward conflict and a life of quest.

His robe was of pure white wool, thrown over a tunic of silk; and a white, pointed cap, with long lapels at the sides, rested on his flowing black hair. It was the dress of the ancient priesthood of the Magi, called the fire-worshippers.

"Welcome!" he said, in his low, pleasant voice, as one after another entered the room--"welcome, Abdus; peace be with you, Rhodaspes and Tigranes, and with you my father, Abgarus. You are all welcome. This house grows bright with the joy of your presence."

There were nine of the men, differing widely in age, but alike in the richness of their dress of many-coloured silks, and in the massive golden collars around their necks, marking them as Parthian nobles, and in the winged circles of gold resting upon their breasts, the sign of the followers of Zoroaster.

They took their places around a small black altar at the end of the room, where a tiny flame was burning. Artaban, standing beside it, and waving a barsom of thin tamarisk branches above the fire, fed it with dry sticks of pine and fragrant oils. Then he began the ancient chant of the Yasna, and the voices of his companions joined in the hymn to Ahura-Mazda:

We worship the Spirit Divine,
    all wisdom and goodness possessing,
Surrounded by Holy Immortals,
    the givers of bounty and blessing;
We joy in the work of His hands,
    His truth and His power confessing.

We praise all the things that are pure,
    for these are His only Creation
The thoughts that are true, and the words

and the deeds that have won approbation;
These are supported by Him,
and for these we make adoration.
Hear us, O Mazda! Thou livest
in truth and in heavenly gladness;
Cleanse us from falsehood, and keep us
from evil and bondage to badness,
Pour out the light and the joy of Thy life
on our darkness and sadness.

Shine on our gardens and fields,
shine on our working and waving;
Shine on the whole race of man,
believing and unbelieving;
Shine on us now through the night,
Shine on us now in Thy might,
The flame of our holy love
and the song of our worship receiving.

The fire rose with the chant, throbbing as if the flame responded to the music, until it cast a bright illumination through the whole apartment, revealing its simplicity and splendour.

The floor was laid with tiles of dark blue veined with white; pilasters of twisted silver stood out against the blue walls; the clear-story of round-arched windows above them was hung with azure silk; the vaulted ceiling was a pavement of blue stones, like the body of heaven in its clearness, sown with silver stars. From the four corners of the roof hung four golden magic-wheels, called the tongues of the gods. At the eastern end, behind the altar, there were two dark-red pillars of porphyry; above them a lintel of the same stone, on which was carved the figure of a winged archer, with his arrow set to the string and his bow drawn.

The doorway between the pillars, which opened upon the terrace of the roof, was covered with a heavy curtain of the colour of a ripe pomegranate, embroidered with innumerable golden rays shooting upward from the floor. In effect the room was like a quiet, starry night, all azure and silver, flushed in the cast with rosy promise of the dawn. It was, as the house of a man should be, an expression of the character and spirit of the master.

He turned to his friends when the song was ended, and invited them to be seated on the divan at the western end of the room.

"You have come to-night," said he, looking around the circle, "at my call, as the faithful scholars of Zoroaster, to renew your worship and rekindle your faith in the God of Purity, even as this fire has been rekindled on the altar. We worship not the fire, but Him of whom it is the chosen symbol, because it is the purest of all created things. It speaks to us of one who is Light and Truth. Is it not so, my father?"

"It is well said, my son," answered the venerable Abgarus. "The enlightened are never idolaters. They lift the veil of form and go in to the shrine of reality, and new light and truth are coming to them continually through the old symbols." "Hear me, then, my father and my friends," said Artaban, "while I tell you of the new light and truth that have come to me through the most ancient of all signs. We have searched the secrets of Nature together, and studied the healing virtues of water and fire and the plants. We have read also the books of prophecy in which the future is dimly foretold in words that are hard to understand. But the highest of all learning is the knowledge of the stars. To trace their course is to untangle the threads of the mystery of life from the beginning to the end. If we could follow them perfectly, nothing would be hidden from us. But is not our knowledge of them still incomplete? Are there not many stars still beyond our horizon--lights that are known only to the dwellers in the far south-land, among the spice-trees of Punt and the gold mines of Ophir?"

There was a murmur of assent among the listeners.

"The stars," said Tigranes, "are the thoughts of the Eternal. They are numberless. But the thoughts of man can be counted, like the years of his life. The wisdom of the Magi is the greatest of all wisdoms on earth, because it knows its own ignorance. And that is the secret of power. We keep men always looking and waiting for a new sunrise. But we ourselves understand that the darkness is equal to the light, and that the conflict between them will never be ended."

"That does not satisfy me," answered Artaban, "for, if the waiting must be endless, if there could be no fulfilment of it, then it would not be wisdom to look and wait. We should become like those new teachers of the Greeks, who say that there is no truth, and that the only wise men are those who spend their lives in discovering and exposing the lies that have been believed in the world. But the new sunrise will certainly appear in the appointed time. Do not our own books tell us that this will come to pass, and that men will see the brightness of a great light?"

"That is true," said the voice of Abgarus; "every faithful disciple of Zoroaster knows the prophecy of the Avesta, and carries the word in his heart. `In that day Sosiosh the Victorious shall arise out of the number of the prophets in the east country. Around him shall shine a mighty brightness, and he shall make life everlasting, incorruptible, and immortal, and the dead shall rise again.'"

"This is a dark saying," said Tigranes, "and it may be that we shall never understand it. It is better to consider the things that are near at hand, and to increase the influence of the Magi in their own country, rather than to look for one who may be a stranger, and to whom we must resign our power."

The others seemed to approve these words. There was a silent feeling of agreement manifest among them; their looks responded with that indefinable expression which always follows when a speaker has uttered the thought that has been slumbering in the hearts of his listeners. But Artaban turned to Abgarus with a glow on his face, and said:

"My father, I have kept this prophecy in the secret place of my soul. Religion without a great hope would be like an altar without a living fire. And now the flame has burned more brightly, and by the light of it I have read other words which also have come from the fountain of Truth, and speak yet more clearly of the rising of the Victorious One in his brightness."

He drew from the breast of his tunic two small rolls of fine parchment, with writing upon them, and unfolded them carefully upon his knee.

"In the years that are lost in the past, long before our fathers came into the land of Babylon, there were wise men in Chaldea, from whom the first of the Magi learned the secret of the heavens. And of these Balaam the son of Beor was one of the mightiest. Hear the words of his prophecy: 'There shall come a star out of Jacob, and a sceptre shall arise out of Israel.'"

The lips of Tigranes drew downward with contempt, as he said:

"Judah was a captive by the waters of Babylon, and the sons of Jacob were in bondage to our kings. The tribes of Israel are scattered through the mountains like lost sheep, and from the remnant that dwells in Judea under the yoke of Rome neither star nor sceptre shall arise."

"And yet," answered Artaban, "it was the Hebrew Daniel, the mighty searcher of dreams, the counsellor of kings, the wise Belteshazzar, who was most honoured and beloved of our great King Cyrus. A prophet of sure things and a reader of the thoughts of the Eternal, Daniel proved himself to our people. And these are the words that he wrote." (Artaban read from the second roll:) " 'Know, therefore, and understand that from the going forth of the commandment to restore Jerusalem, unto the Anointed One, the Prince, the time shall be seven and threescore and two weeks.'"

"But, my son," said Abgarus, doubtfully, "these are mystical numbers. Who can interpret them, or who can find the key that shall unlock their meaning?"

Artaban answered: "It has been shown to me and to my three companions among the Magi--Caspar, Melchior, and Balthazar. We have searched the ancient tablets of Chaldea and computed the time. It falls in this year. We have studied the sky, and in the spring of the year we saw two of the greatest planets draw near together in the sign of the Fish, which is the house of the Hebrews. We also saw a new star there, which shone for one night and then vanished. Now again the two great planets are meeting. This night is their conjunction. My three brothers are watching by the ancient Temple of the Seven Spheres, at Borsippa, in Babylonia, and I am watching here. If the star shines again, they will wait ten days for me at the temple, and then we will set out together for Jerusalem, to see and worship the promised one who shall be born King of Israel. I believe the sign will come. I have made ready for the journey. I have sold my possessions, and bought these three jewels--a sapphire, a ruby, and a pearl--to carry them as tribute to the King. And I ask you to go with me on the pilgrimage, that we may have joy together in finding the Prince who is worthy to be served."

While he was speaking he thrust his hand into the inmost fold of his, girdle and drew out three great gems-- one blue as a fragment of the night sky, one redder than a ray of sunrise, and one as pure as the peak of a snow-mountain at twilight--and laid them on the outspread scrolls before him.

But his friends looked on with strange and alien eyes. A veil of doubt and mistrust came over their faces, like a fog creeping up from the marshes to hide the hills. They glanced at each other with looks of wonder and pity, as those who have listened to incredible sayings, the story of a wild vision, or the proposal of an impossible enterprise.

At last Tigranes said: "Artaban, this is a vain dream. It comes from too much looking upon the stars and the cherishing of lofty thoughts. It would be wiser to spend the time in gathering money for the new fire-temple at Chala. No king will ever rise from the broken race of Israel, and no end will ever come to the eternal strife of light and darkness. He who looks for it is a chaser of shadows. Farewell."

And another said: "Artaban, I have no knowledge of these things, and my office as guardian of the royal treasure binds me here. The quest is not for me. But if thou must follow it, fare thee well."

And another said: "In my house there sleeps a new bride, and I cannot leave her nor take her with me on this strange journey. This quest is not for me. But may thy steps be prospered wherever thou goest. So, farewell."

And another said: "I am ill and unfit for hardship, but there is a man among my servants whom I will send with thee when thou goest, to bring me word how thou farest."

So, one by one, they left the house of Artaban. But Abgarus, the oldest and the one who loved him the best, lingered after the others had gone, and said, gravely: "My son, it may be that the light of truth is in this sign that has appeared in the skies, and then it will surely lead to the Prince and the mighty brightness. Or it may be that it is only a shadow of the light, as Tigranes has said, and then he who follows it will have a long pilgrimage and a fruitless search. But it is better to follow even the shadow of the best than to remain content with the worst. And those who would see wonderful things must often be ready to travel alone. I am too old for this journey, but my heart shall be a companion of thy pilgrimage day and night, and I shall know the end of thy quest. Go in peace."

Then Abgarus went out of the azure chamber with its silver stars, and Artaban was left in solitude.

He gathered up the jewels and replaced them in his girdle. For a long time he stood and watched the flame that flickered and sank upon the altar. Then he crossed the hall, lifted the heavy curtain, and passed out between the pillars of porphyry to the terrace on the roof.

The shiver that runs through the earth ere she rouses from her night-sleep had already begun, and the cool wind that heralds the daybreak was drawing downward from the lofty snow-traced ravines of Mount Orontes. Birds, half-awakened, crept and chirped among the rustling leaves, and the smell of ripened grapes came in brief wafts from the arbours.

Far over the eastern plain a white mist stretched like a lake. But where the distant peaks of Zagros serrated the western horizon the sky was clear. Jupiter and Saturn rolled together like drops of lambent flame about to blend in one.

As Artaban watched them, a steel-blue spark was born out of the darkness beneath, rounding itself with purple splendours to a crimson sphere, and spiring upward through rays of saffron and orange into a point of white radiance. Tiny and infinitely remote, yet perfect in every part, it pulsated in the enormous vault as if the three jewels in the Magian's girdle had mingled and been transformed into a living heart of light.

He bowed his head. He covered his brow with his hands.

"It is the sign," he said. "The King is coming, and I will go to meet him."

II

All night long, Vasda, the swiftest of Artaban's horses, had been waiting, saddled and bridled, in her stall, pawing the ground impatiently, and shaking her bit as if she shared the eagerness of her master's purpose, though she knew not its meaning.

Before the birds had fully roused to their strong, high, joyful chant of morning song, before the white mist had begun to lift lazily from the plain, the Other Wise Man was in the saddle, riding swiftly along the high-road, which skirted the base of Mount Orontes, westward.

How close, how intimate is the comradeship between a man and his favourite horse on a long journey. It is a silent, comprehensive friendship, an intercourse beyond the need of words.

They drink at the same way-side springs, and sleep under the same guardian stars. They are conscious together of the subduing spell of nightfall and the quickening joy of daybreak. The master shares his evening meal with his hungry companion, and feels the soft, moist lips caressing the palm of his hand as they close over the morsel of bread. In the gray dawn he is roused from his bivouac by the gentle stir of a warm, sweet breath over his sleeping face, and looks up into the eyes of his faithful fellow-traveller, ready and waiting for the toil of the day. Surely, unless he is a pagan and an unbeliever, by whatever name he calls upon his God, he will thank Him for this voiceless sympathy, this dumb affection, and his morning prayer will embrace a double blessing-- God bless us both, the horse and the rider, and keep our feet from falling and our souls from death!

Then, through the keen morning air, the swift hoofs beat their tattoo along the road, keeping time to the pulsing of two hearts that are moved with the same eager desire-- to conquer space, to devour the distance, to attain the goal of the journey.

Artaban must indeed ride wisely and well if he would keep the appointed hour with the other Magi; for the route was a hundred and fifty parasangs, and fifteen was the utmost that he could travel in a day. But he knew Vasda's strength, and pushed forward without anxiety, making the fixed distance every day, though he must travel late into the night, and in the morning long before sunrise.

He passed along the brown slopes of Mount Orontes, furrowed by the rocky courses of a hundred torrents.

He crossed the level plains of the Nisaeans, where the famous herds of horses, feeding in the wide pastures, tossed their heads at Vasda's approach, and galloped away with a thunder of many hoofs, and flocks of wild birds rose suddenly from the swampy meadows, wheeling in great circles with a shining flutter of innumerable wings and shrill cries of surprise.

He traversed the fertile fields of Concabar, where the dust from the threshing-floors filled the air with a golden mist, half hiding the huge temple of Astarte with its four hundred pillars.

At Baghistan, among the rich gardens watered by fountains from the rock, he looked up at the mountain thrusting its immense rugged brow out over the road, and saw the figure of King Darius trampling upon his fallen foes, and the proud list of his wars and conquests graven high upon the face of the eternal cliff.

Over many a cold and desolate pass, crawling painfully across the wind-swept shoulders of the hills; down many a black mountain-gorge, where the river roared and raced before him like a savage guide; across many a smiling vale, with terraces of yellow limestone full of vines and fruit-trees; through the oak-groves of Carine and the dark Gates of Zagros, walled in by precipices; into the ancient city of Chala, where the people of Samaria had been kept in captivity long ago; and out again by the mighty portal, riven through the encircling hills, where he saw the image of the High Priest of the Magi sculptured on the wall of rock, with hand uplifted as if to bless the centuries of pilgrims; past the entrance of the narrow defile, filled from end to end with orchards of peaches and figs, through which the river Gyndes foamed down to meet him; over the broad rice-fields, where the autumnal vapours spread their deathly mists; following along the course of the river, under tremulous shadows of poplar and tamarind, among the lower hills; and out upon the flat plain, where the road ran straight as an arrow through the stubble-fields and parched meadows; past the city of Ctesiphon, where the Parthian emperors reigned, and the vast metropolis of Seleucia which Alexander built; across the swirling floods of Tigris and the many channels of Euphrates, flowing yellow through the corn-lands--Artaban pressed onward until he arrived, at nightfall on the tenth day, beneath the shattered walls of populous Babylon.

Vasda was almost spent, and Artaban would gladly have turned into the city to find rest and refreshment for himself and for her. But he knew that it was three hours' journey yet to the Temple of the Seven Spheres, and he must reach the place by midnight if he would find his comrades waiting. So he did not halt, but rode steadily across the stubble-fields.

A grove of date-palms made an island of gloom in the pale yellow sea. As she passed into the shadow Vasda slackened her pace, and began to pick her way more carefully.

Near the farther end of the darkness an access of caution seemed to fall upon her. She scented some danger or difficulty; it was not in her heart to fly from it--only to be prepared for it, and to meet it wisely, as a good horse should do. The grove was close and silent as the tomb; not a leaf rustled, not a bird sang.

She felt her steps before her delicately, carrying her head low, and sighing now and then with apprehension. At last she gave a quick breath of anxiety and dismay, and stood stock-still, quivering in every muscle, before a dark object in the shadow of the last palm-tree.

Artaban dismounted. The dim starlight revealed the form of a man lying across the road. His humble dress and the outline of his haggard face showed that he was probably one of the Hebrews who still dwelt in great numbers around the city. His pallid skin, dry and yellow as parchment, bore the mark of the deadly fever which ravaged the marsh-lands in autumn. The chill of death was in his lean hand, and, as Artaban released it, the arm fell back inertly upon the motionless breast.

He turned away with a thought of pity, leaving the body to that strange burial which the Magians deemed most fitting--the funeral of the desert, from which the kites and vultures rise on dark wings, and the beasts of prey slink furtively away. When they are gone there is only a heap of white bones on the sand.

But, as he turned, a long, faint, ghostly sigh came from the man's lips. The bony fingers gripped the hem of the Magian's robe and held him fast.

Artaban's heart leaped to his throat, not with fear, but with a dumb resentment at the importunity of this blind delay.

How could he stay here in the darkness to minister to a dying stranger? What claim had this unknown fragment of human life upon his compassion or his service? If he lingered but for an hour he could hardly reach Borsippa at the appointed time. His companions would think he had given up the journey. They would go without him. He would lose his quest.

But if he went on now, the man would surely die. If Artaban stayed, life might be restored. His spirit throbbed and fluttered with the urgency of the crisis. Should he risk the great reward of his faith for the sake of a single deed of charity? Should he turn aside, if only for a moment, from the following of the star, to give a cup of cold water to a poor, perishing Hebrew?

"God of truth and purity," he prayed, "direct me in the holy path, the way of wisdom which Thou only knowest."

Then he turned back to the sick man. Loosening the grasp of his hand, he carried him to a little mound at the foot of the palm-tree.

He unbound the thick folds of the turban and opened the garment above the sunken breast. He brought water from one of the small canals near by, and moistened the sufferer's brow and mouth. He mingled a draught of one of those simple but potent remedies which he carried always in his girdle--for the Magians were physicians as well as astrologers--and poured it slowly between the colourless lips. Hour after hour he laboured as only a skilful healer of disease can do. At last the man's strength returned; he sat up and looked about him.

"Who art thou?" he said, in the rude dialect of the country, "and why hast thou sought me here to bring back my life?"

"I am Artaban the Magian, of the city of Ecbatana, and I am going to Jerusalem in search of one who is to be born King of the Jews, a great Prince and Deliverer of all men. I dare not delay any longer upon my journey, for the caravan that has waited for me may depart without me. But see, here is all that I have left of bread and wine, and here is a potion of healing herbs. When thy strength is restored thou canst find the dwellings of the Hebrews among the houses of Babylon."

The Jew raised his trembling hand solemnly to heaven.

"Now may the God of Abraham and Isaac and Jacob bless and prosper the journey of the merciful, and bring him in peace to his desired haven. Stay! I have nothing to give thee in return--only this: that I can tell thee where the Messiah must be sought. For our prophets have said that he should be born not in Jerusalem, but in Bethlehem of Judah. May the Lord bring thee in safety to that place, because thou hast had pity upon the sick."

It was already long past midnight. Artaban rode in haste, and Vasda, restored by the brief rest, ran eagerly through the silent plain and swam the channels of the river. She put forth the remnant of her strength, and fled over the ground like a gazelle.

But the first beam of the rising sun sent a long shadow before her as she entered upon the final stadium of the journey, and the eyes of Artaban, anxiously scanning the great mound of Nimrod and the Temple of the Seven Spheres, could discern no trace of his friends.

The many-coloured terraces of black and orange and red and yellow and green and blue and white, shattered by the convulsions of nature, and crumbling under the repeated blows of human violence, still glittered like a ruined rainbow in the morning light.

Artaban rode swiftly around the hill. He dismounted and climbed to the highest terrace, looking out toward the west.

The huge desolation of the marshes stretched away to the horizon and the border of the desert. Bitterns stood by the stagnant pools and jackals skulked through the low bushes; but there was no sign of the caravan of the Wise Men, far or near.

At the edge of the terrace he saw a little cairn of broken bricks, and under them a piece of papyrus. He caught it up and read: "We have waited past the midnight, and can delay no longer. We go to find the King. Follow us across the desert."

Artaban sat down upon the ground and covered his head in despair.

"How can I cross the desert," said he, "with no food and with a spent horse? I must return to Babylon, sell my sapphire, and buy a train of camels, and provision for the journey. I may never overtake my friends. Only God the merciful knows whether I shall not lose the sight of the King because I tarried to show mercy."

III

There was a silence in the Hall of Dreams, where I was listening to the story of the Other Wise Man. Through this silence I saw, but very dimly, his figure passing over the dreary undulations of the desert, high upon the back of his camel, rocking steadily onward like a ship over the waves.

The land of death spread its cruel net around him. The stony waste bore no fruit but briers and thorns. The dark ledges of rock thrust themselves above the surface here and there, like the bones of perished monsters. Arid and inhospitable mountain-ranges rose before him, furrowed with dry channels of ancient torrents, white and ghastly as scars on the face of nature. Shifting hills of treacherous sand were heaped like tombs along the horizon. By day, the fierce heat pressed its intolerable burden on the quivering air. No living creature moved on the dumb, swooning earth, but tiny jerboas scuttling through the parched bushes, or lizards vanishing in the clefts of the rock. By night the jackals prowled and barked in the distance, and the lion made the black ravines echo with his hollow roaring, while a bitter, blighting chill followed the fever of the day. Through heat and cold, the Magian moved steadily onward.

Then I saw the gardens and orchards of Damascus, watered by the streams of Abana and Pharpar, with their sloping swards inlaid with bloom, and their thickets of myrrh and roses. I saw the long, snowy ridge of Hermon, and the dark groves of cedars, and the valley of the Jordan, and the blue waters of the Lake of Galilee, and the fertile plain of Esdraelon, and the hills of Ephraim, and the highlands of Judah. Through all these I followed the figure of Artaban moving steadily onward, until he arrived at Bethlehem. And it was the third day after the three Wise Men had come to that place and had found Mary and Joseph, with the young child, Jesus, and had laid their gifts of gold and frankincense and myrrh at his feet.

Then the Other Wise Man drew near, weary, but full of hope, bearing his ruby and his pearl to offer to the King. "For now at last," he said, "I shall surely find him, though I be alone, and later than my brethren. This is the place of which the Hebrew exile told me that the prophets had spoken, and here I shall behold the rising of the great light. But I must inquire about the visit of my brethren, and to what house the star directed them, and to whom they presented their tribute."

The streets of the village seemed to be deserted, and Artaban wondered whether the men had all gone up to the hill-pastures to bring down their sheep. From the open door of a cottage he heard the sound of a woman's voice singing softly. He entered and found a young mother hushing her baby to rest. She told him of the strangers from the far East who had appeared in the village three days ago, and how they said that a star had guided them to the place where Joseph of Nazareth was lodging with his wife and her new-born child, and how they had paid reverence to the child and given him many rich gifts.

"But the travellers disappeared again," she continued, "as suddenly as they had come. We were afraid at the strangeness of their visit. We could not understand it. The man of Nazareth took the child and his mother, and fled away that same night secretly, and it was whispered that they were going to Egypt. Ever since, there has been a spell upon the village; something evil hangs over it. They say that the Roman soldiers are coming from

Jerusalem to force a new tax from us, and the men have driven the flocks and herds far back among the hills, and hidden themselves to escape it."

Artaban listened to her gentle, timid speech, and the child in her arms looked up in his face and smiled, stretching out its rosy hands to grasp at the winged circle of gold on his breast. His heart warmed to the touch. It seemed like a greeting of love and trust to one who had journeyed long in loneliness and perplexity, fighting with his own doubts and fears, and following a light that was veiled in clouds.

"Why might not this child have been the promised Prince?" he asked within himself, as he touched its soft cheek. "Kings have been born ere now in lowlier houses than this, and the favourite of the stars may rise even from a cottage. But it has not seemed good to the God of wisdom to reward my search so soon and so easily. The one whom I seek has gone before me; and now I must follow the King to Egypt."

The young mother laid the baby in its cradle, and rose to minister to the wants of the strange guest that fate had brought into her house. She set food before him, the plain fare of peasants, but willingly offered, and therefore full of refreshment for the soul as well as for the body. Artaban accepted it gratefully; and, as he ate, the child fell into a happy slumber, and murmured sweetly in its dreams, and a great peace filled the room.

But suddenly there came the noise of a wild confusion in the streets of the village, a shrieking and wailing of women's voices, a clangour of brazen trumpets and a clashing of swords, and a desperate cry: "The soldiers! the soldiers of Herod! They are killing our children."

The young mother's face grew white with terror. She clasped her child to her bosom, and crouched motionless in the darkest corner of the room, covering him with the folds of her robe, lest he should wake and cry.

But Artaban went quickly and stood in the doorway of the house. His broad shoulders filled the portal from side to side, and the peak of his white cap all but touched the lintel.

The soldiers came hurrying down the street with bloody hands and dripping swords. At the sight of the stranger in his imposing dress they hesitated with surprise. The captain of the band approached the threshold to thrust him aside. But Artaban did not stir. His face was as calm as though he were watching the stars, and in his eyes there burned that steady radiance before which even the half-tamed hunting leopard shrinks, and the bloodhound pauses in his leap. He held the soldier silently for an instant, and then said in a low voice:

"I am all alone in this place, and I am waiting to give this jewel to the prudent captain who will leave me in peace."

He showed the ruby, glistening in the hollow of his hand like a great drop of blood.

The captain was amazed at the splendour of the gem. The pupils of his eyes expanded with desire, and the hard lines of greed wrinkled around his lips. He stretched out his hand and took the ruby.

"March on!" he cried to his men, "there is no child here. The house is empty."

The clamor and the clang of arms passed down the street as the headlong fury of the chase sweeps by the secret covert where the trembling deer is hidden. Artaban re-entered the cottage. He turned his face to the east and prayed:

"God of truth, forgive my sin! I have said the thing that is not, to save the life of a child. And two of my gifts are gone. I have spent for man that which was meant for God. Shall I ever be worthy to see the face of the King?"

But the voice of the woman, weeping for joy in the shadow behind him, said very gently:

"Because thou hast saved the life of my little one, may the Lord bless thee and keep thee; the Lord make His face to shine upon thee and be gracious unto thee; the Lord lift up His countenance upon thee and give thee peace."

IV

Again there was a silence in the Hall of Dreams, deeper and more mysterious than the first interval, and I understood that the years of Artaban were flowing very swiftly under the stillness, and I caught only a glimpse, here and there, of the river of his life shining through the mist that concealed its course.

I saw him moving among the throngs of men in populous Egypt, seeking everywhere for traces of the household that had come down from Bethlehem, and finding them under the spreading sycamore-trees of Heliopolis, and beneath the walls of the Roman fortress of New Babylon beside the Nile--traces so faint and dim that they vanished before him continually, as footprints on the wet river-sand glisten for a moment with moisture and then disappear.

I saw him again at the foot of the pyramids, which lifted their sharp points into the intense saffron glow of the sunset sky, changeless monuments of the perishable glory and the imperishable hope of man. He looked up into the face of the crouching Sphinx and vainly tried to read the meaning of the calm eyes and smiling mouth. Was it, indeed, the mockery of all effort and all aspiration, as Tigranes had said--the cruel jest of a riddle that has no answer, a search that never can succeed? Or was there a touch of pity and encouragement in that inscrutable smile--a promise that even the defeated should attain a victory, and the disappointed should discover a prize, and the ignorant should be made wise, and the blind should see, and the wandering should come into the haven at last?

I saw him again in an obscure house of Alexandria, taking counsel with a Hebrew rabbi. The venerable man, bending over the rolls of parchment on which the prophecies of Israel were written, read aloud the pathetic words which foretold the sufferings of the promised Messiah--the despised and rejected of men, the man of sorrows and acquainted with grief.

"And remember, my son," said he, fixing his eyes upon the face of Artaban, "the King whom thou seekest is not to be found in a palace, nor among the rich and powerful. If the light of the world and the glory of Israel had been appointed to come with the greatness of earthly splendour, it must have appeared long ago. For no son of Abraham will ever again rival the power which Joseph had in the palaces of Egypt, or the magnificence of Solomon throned between the lions in Jerusalem. But the light for which the world is waiting is a new light, the glory that shall rise out of patient and triumphant suffering. And the kingdom which is to be established forever is a new kingdom, the royalty of unconquerable love.

"I do not know how this shall come to pass, nor how the turbulent kings and peoples of earth shall be brought to acknowledge the Messiah and pay homage to him. But this I know. Those who seek him will do well to look among the poor and the lowly, the sorrowful and the oppressed."

So I saw the Other Wise Man again and again, travelling from place to place, and searching among the people of the dispersion, with whom the little family from Bethlehem might, perhaps, have found a refuge. He passed through countries where famine lay heavy upon the land, and the poor were crying for bread. He made his dwelling in plague-stricken cities where the sick were languishing in the bitter companionship of helpless misery. He visited the oppressed and the afflicted in the gloom of subterranean prisons, and the crowded wretchedness of slave-markets, and the weary toil of galley-ships. In all this populous and intricate world of anguish, though he found none to worship, he found many to help. He fed the hungry, and clothed the naked, and healed the sick, and comforted the captive; and his years passed more swiftly than the weaver's shuttle that flashes back and forth through the loom while the web grows and the pattern is completed.

It seemed almost as if he had forgotten his quest. But once I saw him for a moment as he stood alone at sunrise, waiting at the gate of a Roman prison. He had taken from a secret resting-place in his bosom the pearl, the last of his jewels. As he looked at it, a mellower lustre, a soft and iridescent light, full of shifting gleams of azure and rose, trembled upon its surface. It seemed to have absorbed some reflection of the lost sapphire and ruby. So the secret purpose of a noble life draws into itself the memories of past joy and past sorrow. All that has helped it, all that has hindered it, is transfused by a subtle magic into its very essence. It becomes more luminous and precious the longer it is carried close to the warmth of the beating heart.

Then, at last, while I was thinking of this pearl, and of its meaning, I heard the end of the story of the Other Wise Man.

V

Three-and-thirty years of the life of Artaban had passed away, and he was still a pilgrim and a seeker after light. His hair, once darker than the cliffs of Zagros, was now white as the wintry snow that covered them. His eyes, that once flashed like flames of fire, were dull as embers smouldering among the ashes.

Worn and weary and ready to die, but still looking for the King, he had come for the last time to Jerusalem. He had often visited the holy city before, and had searched all its lanes and crowded bevels and black prisons without finding any trace of the family of Nazarenes who had fled from Bethlehem long ago. But now it seemed as if he must make one more effort, and something whispered in his heart that, at last, he might succeed.

It was the season of the Passover. The city was thronged with strangers. The children of Israel, scattered in far lands, had returned to the Temple for the great feast, and there had been a confusion of tongues in the narrow streets for many days.

But on this day a singular agitation was visible in the multitude. The sky was veiled with a portentous gloom. Currents of excitement seemed to flash through the crowd. A secret tide was sweeping them all one way. The clatter of sandals and the soft, thick sound of thousands of bare feet shuffling over the stones, flowed unceasingly along the street that leads to the Damascus gate.

Artaban joined a group of people from his own country, Parthian Jews who had come up to keep the Passover, and inquired of them the cause of the tumult, and where they were going.

"We are going," they answered, "to the place called Golgotha, outside the city walls, where there is to be an execution. Have you not heard what has happened? Two famous robbers are to be crucified, and with them another, called Jesus of Nazareth, a man who has done many wonderful works among the people, so that they love him greatly. But the priests and elders have said that he must die, because he gave himself out to be the Son of God. And Pilate has sent him to the cross because he said that he was the `King of the Jews.'

How strangely these familiar words fell upon the tired heart of Artaban! They had led him for a lifetime over land and sea. And now they came to him mysteriously, like a message of despair. The King had arisen, but he had been denied and cast out. He was about to perish. Perhaps he was already dying. Could it be the same who had been born in Bethlehem thirty-three years ago, at whose birth the star had appeared in heaven, and of whose coming the prophets had spoken?

Artaban's heart beat unsteadily with that troubled, doubtful apprehension which is the excitement of old age. But he said within himself: "The ways of God are stranger than the thoughts of men, and it may be that I shall find the King, at last, in the hands of his enemies, and shall come in time to offer my pearl for his ransom before he dies."

So the old man followed the multitude with slow and painful steps toward the Damascus gate of the city. Just beyond the entrance of the guardhouse a troop of Macedonian soldiers came down the street, dragging a young girl with torn dress and dishevelled hair. As the Magian paused to look at her with compassion, she broke suddenly from the hands of her tormentors, and threw herself at his feet, clasping him around the knees. She had seen his white cap and the winged circle on his breast.

"Have pity on me," she cried, "and save me, for the sake of the God of Purity! I also am a daughter of the true religion which is taught by the Magi. My father was a merchant of Parthia, but he is dead, and I am seized for his debts to be sold as a slave. Save me from worse than death!"

Artaban trembled.

It was the old conflict in his soul, which had come to him in the palm-grove of Babylon and in the cottage at Bethlehem--the conflict between the expectation of faith and the impulse of love. Twice the gift which he had consecrated to the worship of religion had been drawn to the service of humanity. This was the third trial, the ultimate probation, the final and irrevocable choice.

Was it his great opportunity, or his last temptation? He could not tell. One thing only was clear in the darkness of his mind--it was inevitable. And does not the inevitable come from God?

One thing only was sure to his divided heart--to rescue this helpless girl would be a true deed of love. And is not love the light of the soul?

He took the pearl from his bosom. Never had it seemed so luminous, so radiant, so full of tender, living lustre. He laid it in the hand of the slave.

"This is thy ransom, daughter! It is the last of my treasures which I kept for the King."

While he spoke, the darkness of the sky deepened, and shuddering tremors ran through the earth heaving convulsively like the breast of one who struggles with mighty grief.

The walls of the houses rocked to and fro. Stones were loosened and crashed into the street. Dust clouds filled the air. The soldiers fled in terror, reeling like drunken men. But Artaban and the girl whom he had ransomed crouched helpless beneath the wall of the Praetorium.

What had he to fear? What had he to hope? He had given away the last remnant of his tribute for the King. He had parted with the last hope of finding him. The quest was over, and it had failed. But, even in that thought, accepted and embraced, there was peace. It was not resignation. It was not submission. It was something more profound and searching. He knew that all was well, because he had done the best that he could from day to day. He had been true to the light that had been given to him. He had looked for more. And if he had not found it, if a failure was all that came out of his life, doubtless that was the best that was possible. He had not seen the revelation of "life everlasting, incorruptible and immortal." But he knew that even if he could live his earthly life over again, it could not be otherwise than it had been.

One more lingering pulsation of the earthquake quivered through the ground. A heavy tile, shaken from the roof, fell and struck the old man on the temple. He lay breathless and pale, with his gray head resting on the young girl's shoulder, and the blood trickling from the wound. As she bent over him, fearing that he was dead, there came a voice through the twilight, very small and still, like music sounding from a distance, in which the notes are clear but the words are lost. The girl turned to see if some one had spoken from the window above them, but she saw no one.

Then the old man's lips began to move, as if in answer, and she heard him say in the Parthian tongue:

"Not so, my Lord! For when saw I thee an hungered and fed thee? Or thirsty, and gave thee drink? When saw I thee a stranger, and took thee in? Or naked, and clothed thee? When saw I thee sick or in prison, and came unto thee? Three-and-- thirty years have I looked for thee; but I have never seen thy face, nor ministered to thee, my King."

He ceased, and the sweet voice came again. And again the maid heard it, very faint and far away. But now it seemed as though she understood the words:

"Verily I say unto thee, Inasmuch as thou hast done it unto one of the least of these my brethren, thou hast done it unto me."

A calm radiance of wonder and joy lighted the pale face of Artaban like the first ray of dawn, on a snowy mountain-peak. A long breath of relief exhaled gently from his lips.

His journey was ended. His treasures were accepted. The Other Wise Man had found the King.

The Burglar's Christmas.

By

Elizabeth L. Seymour.

TWO very shabby looking young men stood at the corner of Prairie avenue and Eightieth street, looking despondently at the carriages that whirled by. It was Christmas Eve, and the streets were full of vehicles; florists' wagons, grocers' carts and car-riages. The streets were in that half-liquid, half-congealed condition peculiar to the streets of Chicago at that season of the year. The swift wheels that spun by sometimes threw the slush of mud and snow over the two young men who were talking on the corner.

"Well," remarked the elder of the two, "I guess we are at our rope's end, sure enough. How do you feel?"

"Pretty shaky. The wind's sharp to-night. If I had had anything to eat I mightn't mind it so much. There is simply no show. I'm sick of the whole business. Looks like there's nothing for it but the lake."

"O, nonsense, I thought you had more grit. Got anything left you can hoc?"

"Nothing but my beard, and I am afraid they wouldn't find it worth a pawn ticket," said the younger man ruefully, rubbing the week's growth of stubble on his face.

"Got any folks anywhere? Now's your time to strike 'em if you have."

"Never mind if I have, they're out of the question."

"Well, you'll be out of it before many hours if you don't make a move of some sort. A man's got to eat. See here, I am going down to Longtin's saloon. I used to play the banjo in there with a couple of coons, and I'll bone him for some of his free lunch stuff. You'd better come along, perhaps they'll fill an order for two."

"How far down is it?"

"Well, it's clear down town, of course, way down on Michigan avenue."

"Thanks, I guess I'll loaf around here. I don't feel equal to the walk, and the cars—well, the cars are crowded." His features drew themselves into what might have been a smile under happier circumstances.

"No, you never did like street cars, you're too aristocratic. See here, Crawford, I don't like leaving you here. You ain't good company for yourself to-night."

"Crawford? O, yes, that's the last one. There have been so many I forget them."

"Have you got a real name, anyway?"

"O, yes, but it's one of the ones I've forgotten. Don't you worry about me. You go along and get your free lunch. I think I had a row in Longtin's place once. I'd better not show myself there again." As he spoke the young man nodded and turned slowly up the avenue.

He was miserable enough to want to be quite alone. Even the crowd that jostled by him annoyed him. He wanted to think about himself. He had avoided this final reckoning with himself for a year now. He had laughed it off and drunk it off. But now, when all those artificial devices which are employed to turn our thoughts into other channels and shield us from ourselves had failed him, it must come. Hunger is a powerful incentive to introspection.

It is a tragic hour, that hour when we are finally driven to reckon with ourselves, when every avenue of mental distraction has been cut off and our own life and all its ineffaceable failures closes about us like the walls of that old torture chamber of the Inquisition. To-night, as this man stood stranded in the streets of the city, his hour came. It was not the first time he had been hungry and desperate and alone. But always before there had been some outlook, some chance ahead, some pleasure yet untasted that seemed worth the effort, some face that he fancied was, or would be, dear. But it was not so to-night. The unyielding conviction was upon him that he had failed in everything, had outlived everything. It had been near him for a long time, that Pale Spectre. He had caught its shadow at the bottom of his glass many a time, at the head of his bed when he was sleepless at night, in the twilight shadows when some great sunset broke upon him. It had made life hateful to him when he awoke in the morning before now. But now it settled slowly over him, like night, the endless Northern nights that bid the sun a long farewell. It rose up before him like granite. From this brilliant city with its glad bustle of Yule-tide he was shut off as completely as though he were a creature of another species. His days seemed numbered and done, sealed over like the little coral cells at the bottom of the sea. Involuntarily he drew that cold air through his lungs slowly, as though he were tasting it for the last time.

Yet he was but four and twenty, this man—he looked even younger—and he had a father some place down East who had been very proud of him once. Well, he had taken his life into his own hands, and this was what he had made of it. That was all there was to be said. He could remember the hopeful things they used to say about him at college in the old days, before he had cut away and begun to live by his wits, and he found courage to smile at them now. They had read him wrongly. He knew now that he never had the essentials of success, only the superficial agility that is often mistaken for it. He was tow without the tinder, and he had burnt himself out at other people's fires. He had helped other people to make it win, but he himself—he had never touched an enterprise that had not failed eventually. Or, if it survived his connection with it, it left him behind.

His last venture had been with some ten-cent specialty company, a little lower than all the others, that had gone to pieces in Buffalo, and he had worked his way to Chicago by boat. When the boat made up its crew for the outward voyage, he was dispensed with as usual. He was used to that. The reason for it? O, there are so many reasons for failure! His was a very common one.

As he stood there in the wet under the street light he drew up his reckoning with the world and decided that it had treated him as well as he deserved. He had overdrawn his account once too often. There had been a day when he thought otherwise; when he had said he was unjustly handled, that his failure was merely the lack of proper adjustment between himself and other men, that some day he would be recognized and it would all come right. But he knew better than that now, and he was still man enough to bear no grudge against any one—man or woman.

To-night was his birthday, too. There seemed something particularly amusing in that. He turned up a limp little coat collar to try to keep a little of the wet chill from his throat, and instinctively began to remember all the birthday parties he used to have. He was so cold and empty that his mind seemed unable to grapple with any serious question. He kept thinking about ginger bread and frosted cakes like a child. He could remember the splendid birthday parties his mother used to give him, when all the other little boys in the block came in their Sunday clothes and creaking shoes, with their ears still red from their mother's towel, and the pink and white birthday cake, and the stuffed olives and all the dishes of which he had been particularly fond, and how he would eat and eat and then go to bed and dream of Santa Claus. And in the morning he would awaken and eat again, until by night the family doctor arrived with his castor oil, and poor William used to dolefully say that it was altogether too much to have your birthday and Christmas all at once. He could remember, too, the royal birthday suppers he had given at college, and the stag dinners, and the toasts, and the music, and the good fellows who had wished him happiness and really meant what they said.

And since then there were other birthday suppers that he could not remember so clearly; the memory of them was heavy and flat, like cigarette smoke that has been shut in a room all night, like champagne that has been a day opened, a song that has been too often sung, an acute sensation that has been overstrained. They seemed tawdry and garish, discordant to him now. He rather wished he could forget them altogether.

Whichever way his mind now turned there was one thought that it could not escape, and that was the idea of food. He caught the scent of a cigar suddenly, and felt a sharp pain in the pit of his abdomen and a sudden moisture in his mouth. His cold hands clenched angrily, and for a moment he felt that bitter hatred of wealth, of ease, of everything that is well-fed and well-housed that is common to starving men. At any rate he had a right to eat! He had demanded great things from the world once: fame and wealth and admiration. Now it was simply bread—and he would have it! He looked about him quickly and felt the blood begin to stir in his veins. In all his straits he had never stolen anything, his tastes were above it. But to-night there would be no to-morrow. He was amused at the way in which the idea excited him. Was it possible there was yet one more experience that would distract him, one thing that had power to excite his jaded interest? Good! he had failed at everything else, now he would see what his chances would be as a common thief. It would be amusing to watch the beautiful consistency of his destiny work itself out even in that role. It would be interesting to add another study to his gallery of futile attempts, and then label them all: "the failure as a journalist," "the failure as a lecturer," "the failure as a business man," "the failure as a thief," and so on, like the titles under the pictures of the Dance of Death. It was time that Childe Roland came to the dark tower.

A girl hastened by him with her arms full of packages. She walked quickly and nervously, keeping well within the shadow, as if she were not accustomed to carrying bundles and did not care to meet any of her friends. As she crossed the muddy street, she made an effort to lift her skirt a little, and as she did so one of the packages slipped unnoticed from beneath her arm. He caught it up and overtook her. "Excuse me, but I think you dropped something."

She started, "O, yes, thank you, I would rather have lost anything than that."

The young man turned angrily upon himself. The package must have contained something of value. Why had he not kept it? Was this the sort of thief he would make? He ground his teeth together. There is nothing more maddening than to have morally consented to crime and then lack the nerve force to carry it out.

A carriage drove up to the house before which he stood. Several richly dressed women alighted and went in. It was a new house, and must have been built since he was in Chicago last. The front door was open and he could see down the hall-way and up the stair case. The servant had left the door and gone with the guests. The first floor was brilliantly lighted, but the windows upstairs were dark. It looked very easy, just to slip upstairs to the darkened chambers where the jewels and trinkets of the fashionable occupants were kept.

Still burning with impatience against himself he entered quickly. Instinctively he removed his mud-stained hat as he passed quickly and quietly up the stair case. It struck him as being a rather superfluous courtesy in a burglar, but he had done it before he had thought. His way was clear enough, he met no one on the stairway or in the upper hall. The gas was lit in the upper hall. He passed the first chamber door through sheer cowardice. The second he entered quickly, thinking of something else lest his courage should fail him, and closed the door behind him. The light from the hall shone into the room through the transom. The apartment was furnished richly enough to justify his expectations. He went at once to the dressing case. A number of rings and small trinkets lay in a silver tray. These he put hastily in his pocket. He opened the upper drawer and found, as he expected, several leather cases. In the first he opened was a lady's watch, in the second a pair of old-fashioned bracelets; he seemed to dimly remember having seen bracelets like them before, somewhere. The third case was heavier, the spring was much worn, and it opened easily. It held a cup of some kind. He held it up to the light and then his strained nerves gave way and he uttered a sharp exclamation. It was the silver mug he used to drink from when he was a little boy.

The door opened, and a woman stood in the doorway facing him. She was a tall woman, with white hair, in evening dress. The light from the hall streamed in upon him, but she was not afraid. She stood looking at him a moment, then she threw out her hand and went quickly toward him.

"Willie, Willie! Is it you!"

He struggled to loose her arms from him, to keep her lips from his cheek. "Mother—you must not! You do not understand! O, my God, this is worst of all!" Hunger, weakness, cold, shame, all came back to him, and shook his self-control completely. Physically he was too weak to stand a shock like this. Why could it not have been an ordinary discovery, arrest, the station house and all the rest of it. Anything but this! A hard dry sob broke from him. Again he strove to disengage himself.

"Who is it says I shall not kiss my son? O, my boy, we have waited so long for this! You have been so long in coming, even I almost gave you up."

Her lips upon his cheek burnt him like fire. He put his hand to his throat, and spoke thickly and incoherently: "You do not understand. I did not know you were here. I came here to rob—it is the first time—I swear it—but I am a common thief. My pockets are full of your jewels now. Can't you hear me? I am a common thief!"

"Hush, my boy, those are ugly words. How could you rob your own house? How could you take what is your own? They are all yours, my son, as wholly yours as my great love—and you can't doubt that, Will, do you?"

That soft voice, the warmth and fragrance of her person stole through his chill, empty veins like a gentle stimulant. He felt as though all his strength were leaving him and even consciousness. He held fast to her and bowed his head on her strong shoulder, and groaned aloud.

"O, mother, life is hard, hard!"

She said nothing, but held him closer. And O, the strength of those white arms that held him! O, the assurance of safety in that warm bosom that rose and fell under his cheek! For a moment they stood so, silently. Then they heard a heavy step upon the stair. She led him to a chair and went out and closed the door. At the top of the staircase she met a tall, broad-shouldered man, with iron gray hair, and a face alert and stern. Her eyes were shining and her cheeks on fire, her whole face was one expression of intense determination.

"James, it is William in there, come home. You must keep him at any cost. If he goes this time, I go with him. O, James, be easy with him, he has suffered so." She broke from a command to an entreaty, and laid her hand on his shoulder. He looked questioningly at her a moment, then went in the room and quietly shut the door.

She stood leaning against the wall, clasping her temples with her hands and listening to the low indistinct sound of the voices within. Her own lips moved silently. She waited a long time, scarcely breathing. At last the door opened, and her husband came out. He stopped to say in a shaken voice,

"You go to him now, he will stay. I will go to my room. I will see him again in the morning."

She put her arm about his neck, "O, James, I thank you, I thank you! This is the night he came so long ago, you remember? I gave him to you then, and now you give him back to me!"

"Don't, Helen," he muttered. "He is my son, I have never forgotten that. I failed with him. I don't like to fail, it cuts my pride. Take him and make a man of him." He passed on down the hall.

She flew into the room where the young man sat with his head bowed upon his knee. She dropped upon her knees beside him. Ah, it was so good to him to feel those arms again!

"He is so glad, Willie, so glad! He may not show it, but he is as happy as I. He never was demonstrative with either of us, you know."

"O, my God, he was good enough," groaned the man. "I told him everything, and he was good enough. I don't see how either of you can look at me, speak to me, touch me." He shivered under her clasp again as when she had first touched him, and tried weakly to throw her off.

But she whispered softly,

"This is my right, my son."

Presently, when he was calmer, she rose. "Now, come with me into the library, and I will have your dinner brought there."

As they went down stairs she remarked apologetically, "I will not call Ellen to-night; she has a number of guests to attend to. She is a big girl now, you know, and came out last winter. Besides, I want you all to myself to-night."

When the dinner came, and it came very soon, he fell upon it savagely. As he ate she told him all that had transpired during the years of his absence, and how his father's business had brought them there. "I was glad when we came. I thought you would drift West. I seemed a good deal nearer to you here."

There was a gentle unobtrusive sadness in her tone that was too soft for a reproach.

"Have you everything you want? It is a comfort to see you eat."

He smiled grimly, "It is certainly a comfort to me. I have not indulged in this frivolous habit for some thirty-five hours."

She caught his hand and pressed it sharply, uttering a quick remonstrance.

"Don't say that! I know, but I can't hear you say it,—it's too terrible! My boy, food has choked me many a time when I have thought of the possibility of that. Now take the old lounging chair by the fire, and if you are too tired to talk, we will just sit and rest together."

He sank into the depths of the big leather chair with the lion's heads on the arms, where he had sat so often in the days when his feet did not touch the floor and he was half afraid of the grim monsters cut in the polished wood. That chair seemed to speak to him of things long forgotten. It was like the touch of an old familiar friend. He felt a sudden yearning tenderness for the happy little boy who had sat there and dreamed of the big world so long ago. Alas, he had been dead many a summer, that little boy!

He sat looking up at the magnificent woman beside him. He had almost forgotten how handsome she was; how lustrous and sad were the eyes that were set under that serene brow, how impetuous and wayward the mouth even now, how superb the white throat and shoulders! Ah, the wit and grace and fineness of this woman! He remembered how proud he had been of her as a boy when she came to see him at school. Then in the deep red coals of the grate he saw the faces of other women who had come since then into his vexed, disordered life. Laughing faces, with eyes artificially bright, eyes without depth or meaning, features without the stamp of high sensibilities. And he had left this face for such as those!

He sighed restlessly and laid his hand on hers. There seemed refuge and protection in the touch of her, as in the old days when he was afraid of the dark. He had been in the dark so long now, his confidence was so thoroughly shaken, and he was bitterly afraid of the night and of himself.

"Ah, mother, you make other things seem so false. You must feel that I owe you an explanation, but I can't make any, even to myself. Ah, but we make poor exchanges in life. I can't make out the riddle of it all. Yet there are things I ought to tell you before I accept your confidence like this."

"I'd rather you wouldn't, Will. Listen: Between you and me there can be no secrets. We are more alike than other people. Dear boy, I know all about it. I am a woman, and circumstances were different with me, but we are of one blood. I have lived all your life before you. You have never had an impulse that I have not known, you have never touched a brink that my feet have not trod. This is your birthday night. Twenty-four years ago I foresaw all this. I was a young woman then and I had hot battles of my own, and I felt your likeness to me. You were not like other babies. From the hour you were born you were restless and discontented, as I had been before you. You used to brace your strong little limbs against mine and try to throw me off as you did to-night. To-night you have come back to me, just as you always did after you ran away to swim in the river that was forbidden you, the river you loved because it was forbidden. You are tired and sleepy, just as you used to be then, only a little older and a little paler and a little more foolish. I never asked you where you had been then, nor will I now. You have come back to me, that's all in all to me. I know your every possibility and limitation, as a composer knows his instrument."

He found no answer that was worthy to give to talk like this. He had not found life easy since he had lived by his wits. He had come to know poverty at close quarters. He had known what it was to be gay with an empty pocket, to wear violets in his button hole when he had not breakfasted, and all the hateful shams of the poverty of idleness. He had been a reporter on a big metropolitan daily, where men grind out their brains on paper until they have not one idea left—and still grind on. He had worked in a real estate office, where ignorant men were swindled. He had sung in a comic opera chorus and played *Harris* in an Uncle Tom's Cabin Company, and edited a Socialist weekly. He had been dogged by debt and hunger and grinding poverty, until to sit here by a warm fire without concern as to how it would be paid for seemed unnatural.

He looked up at her questioningly. "I wonder if you know how much you pardon?"

"O, my poor boy, much or little, what does it matter? Have you wandered so far and paid such a bitter price for knowledge and not yet learned that love has nothing to do with pardon or forgiveness, that it only loves, and loves—and loves? They have not taught you well, the women of your world." She leaned over and kissed him, as no woman had kissed him since he left her.

He drew a long sigh of rich content. The old life, with all its bitterness and useless antagonism and flimsy sophistries, its brief delights that were always tinged with fear and distrust and unfaith, that whole miserable, futile, swindled world of Bohemia seemed immeasurably distant and far away, like a dream that is over and done. And as the chimes rang joyfully outside and sleep pressed heavily upon his eyelids, he wondered dimly if the Author of this sad little riddle of ours were not able to solve it after all, and if the Potter would not finally mete out his all comprehensive justice, such as none but he could have, to his Things of Clay, which are made in his own patterns, weak or strong, for his own ends; and if some day we will not awaken and find that all evil is a dream, a mental distortion that will pass when the dawn shall break.

The Christmas Banquet

By

Nathaniel Hawthorne

"I have here attempted," said Roderick, unfolding a few sheets of manuscript, as he sat with Rosina and the sculptor in the summer-house,—"I have attempted to seize hold of a personage who glides past me, occasionally, in my walk through life. My former sad experience, as you know, has gifted me with some degree of insight into the gloomy mysteries of the human heart, through which I have wandered like one astray in a dark cavern, with his torch fast flickering to extinction. But this man, this class of men, is a hopeless puzzle."

"Well, but propound him," said the sculptor. "Let us have an idea of hint, to begin with."

"Why, indeed," replied Roderick, "he is such a being as I could conceive you to carve out of marble, and some yet unrealized perfection of human science to endow with an exquisite mockery of intellect; but still there lacks the last inestimable touch of a divine Creator. He looks like a man; and, perchance, like a better specimen of man than you ordinarily meet. You might esteem him wise; he is capable of cultivation and refinement, and has at least an external conscience; but the demands that spirit makes upon spirit are precisely those to which he cannot respond. When at last you come close to him you find him chill and unsubstantial,—a mere vapor."

"I believe," said Rosina, "I have a glimmering idea of what you mean."

"Then be thankful," answered her husband, smiling; "but do not anticipate any further illumination from what I am about to read. I have here imagined such a man to be—what, probably, he never is—conscious of the deficiency in his spiritual organization. Methinks the result would be a sense of cold unreality wherewith he would go shivering through the world, longing to exchange his load of ice for any burden of real grief that fate could fling upon a human being."

Contenting himself with this preface, Roderick began to read.

In a certain old gentleman's last will and testament there appeared a bequest, which, as his final thought and deed, was singularly in keeping with a long life of melancholy eccentricity. He devised a considerable sum for establishing a fund, the interest of which was to be expended, annually forever, in preparing a Christmas Banquet for ten of the most miserable persons that could be found. It seemed not to be the testator's purpose to make these half a score of sad hearts merry, but to provide that the stern or fierce expression of human discontent should not be drowned, even for that one holy and joyful day, amid the acclamations of festal gratitude which all Christendom sends up. And he desired, likewise, to perpetuate his own remonstrance against the earthly course of Providence, and his sad and sour dissent from those systems of religion or philosophy which either find sunshine in the world or draw it down from heaven.

The task of inviting the guests, or of selecting among such as might advance their claims to partake of this dismal hospitality, was confided to the two trustees or stewards of the fund. These gentlemen, like their deceased friend, were sombre humorists, who made it their principal occupation to number the sable threads in the web of human life, and drop all the golden ones out of the reckoning. They performed their present office with integrity and judgment. The aspect of the assembled company, on the day of the first festival, might not, it is true, have satisfied every beholder that these were especially the individuals, chosen forth from all the world, whose griefs were worthy to stand as indicators of the mass of human suffering. Yet, after due consideration, it could not be disputed that here was a variety of hopeless discomfort, which, if it sometimes arose from causes apparently inadequate, was thereby only the shrewder imputation against the nature and mechanism of life.

The arrangements and decorations of the banquet were probably intended to signify that death in life which had been the testator's definition of existence. The hall, illuminated by torches, was hung round with curtains of deep and dusky purple, and adorned with branches of cypress and wreaths of artificial flowers, imitative of such as used to be strewn over the dead. A sprig of parsley was laid by every plate. The main reservoir of wine, was a sepulchral urn of silver, whence the liquor was distributed around the table in small vases, accurately copied from those that held the tears of ancient mourners. Neither had the stewards—if it were their taste that arranged these details—forgotten the fantasy of the old Egyptians, who seated a skeleton at every festive board, and mocked their own merriment with the imperturbable grin of a death's-head. Such a fearful guest, shrouded in a black mantle, sat now at the head of the table. It was whispered, I know not with what truth, that the testator himself had once walked the visible world with the machinery of that sane skeleton, and that it was one of the stipulations of his will, that he should thus be permitted to sit, from year to year, at the banquet which he had instituted. If so, it was perhaps covertly implied that he had cherished no hopes of bliss beyond the grave to compensate for the evils which he felt or imagined here. And if, in their bewildered conjectures as to the purpose of earthly existence, the banqueters should throw aside the veil, and cast an inquiring glance at this figure of death, as seeking thence the solution otherwise unattainable, the only reply would be a stare of the vacant eye-caverns and a grin of the skeleton jaws. Such was the response that the dead man had fancied himself to receive when he asked of Death to solve the riddle of his life; and it was his desire to repeat it when the guests of his dismal hospitality should find themselves perplexed with the same question.

"What means that wreath?" asked several of the company, while viewing the decorations of the table.

They alluded to a wreath of cypress, which was held on high by a skeleton arm, protruding from within the black mantle.

"It is a crown," said one of the stewards, "not for the worthiest, but for the wofulest, when he shall prove his claim to it."

The guest earliest bidden to the festival was a man of soft and gentle character, who had not energy to struggle against the heavy despondency to which his temperament rendered him liable; and therefore with nothing outwardly to excuse him from happiness, he had spent a life of quiet misery that made his blood torpid, and weighed upon his breath, and sat like a ponderous night-fiend upon every throb of his unresisting heart. His wretchedness seemed as deep as his original nature, if not identical with it. It was the misfortune of a second guest to cherish within his bosom a diseased heart, which had become so wretchedly sore that the continual and unavoidable rubs of the world, the blow of an enemy, the careless jostle of a stranger, and even the faithful and loving touch of a friend, alike made ulcers in it. As is the habit of people thus afflicted, he found his chief employment in exhibiting these miserable sores to any who would give themselves the pain of viewing them. A third guest was a hypochondriac, whose imagination wrought necromancy in his outward and inward world, and caused him to see monstrous faces in the household fire, and dragons in the clouds of sunset, and fiends in the guise of beautiful women, and something ugly or wicked beneath all the pleasant surfaces of nature. His neighbor at table was one who, in his early youth, had trusted mankind too much, and hoped too highly in their behalf, and, in meeting with many disappointments, had become desperately soured. For several years back this misanthrope bad employed himself in accumulating motives for hating and despising his race,—such as murder, lust, treachery, ingratitude, faithlessness of trusted friends, instinctive vices of children, impurity of women, hidden guilt in men of saint-like aspect,—and, in short, all manner of black realities that sought to decorate themselves with outward grace or glory. But at every atrocious fact that was added to his catalogue, at every increase of the sad knowledge which he spent his life to collect, the native impulses of the poor man's loving and confiding heart made him groan with anguish. Next, with his heavy brow bent downward, there stole into the hall a man naturally earnest and impassioned, who, from his immemorial infancy, had felt the consciousness of a high message to the world; but, essaying to deliver it, had found either no voice or form of speech, or else no ears to listen. Therefore his whole life was a bitter questioning of himself: "Why have not men acknowledged my mission?

Am I not a self-deluding fool? What business have I on earth? Where is my grave?" Throughout the festival, he quaffed frequent draughts from the sepulchral urn of wine, hoping thus to quench the celestial fire that tortured his own breast and could not benefit his race.

Then there entered, having flung away a ticket for a ball, a gay gallant of yesterday, who had found four or five wrinkles in his brow, and more gray hairs than he could well number on his head. Endowed with sense and feeling, he had nevertheless spent his youth in folly, but had reached at last that dreary point in life where Folly quits us of her own accord, leaving us to make friends with Wisdom if we can. Thus, cold and desolate, he had come to seek Wisdom at the banquet, and wondered if the skeleton were she. To eke out the company, the stewards had invited a distressed poet from his home in the almshouse, and a melancholy idiot from the street-corner. The latter had just the glimmering of sense that was sufficient to make him conscious of a vacancy, which the poor fellow, all his life long, had mistily sought to fill up with intelligence, wandering up and down the streets, and groaning miserably because his attempts were ineffectual. The only lady in the hall was one who had fallen short of absolute and perfect beauty, merely by the trifling defect of a slight cast in her left eye. But this blemish, minute as it was, so shocked the pure ideal of her soul, rather than her vanity, that she passed her life in solitude, and veiled her countenance even from her own gaze. So the skeleton sat shrouded at one end of the table, and this poor lady at the other.

One other guest remains to be described. He was a young man of smooth brow, fair cheek, and fashionable mien. So far as his exterior developed him, he might much more suitably have found a place at some merry Christmas table, than have been numbered among the blighted, fate-stricken, fancy-tortured set of ill-starred banqueters. Murmurs arose among the guests as they noted, the glance of general scrutiny which the intruder threw over his companions. What had he to do among them? Why did not the skeleton of the dead founder of the feast unbend its rattling joints, arise, and motion the unwelcome stranger from the board?

"Shameful!" said the morbid man, while a new ulcer broke out in his heart. "He comes to mock us! we shall be the jest of his tavern friends I—he will make a farce of our miseries, and bring it out upon the stage!"

"O, never mind him!" said the hypochondriac, smiling sourly. "He shall feast from yonder tureen of viper-soup; and if there is a fricassee of scorpions on the table, pray let him have his share of it. For the dessert, he shall taste the apples of Sodom, then, if he like our Christmas fare, let him return again next year!"

"Trouble him not," murmured the melancholy man, with gentleness. "What matters it whether the consciousness of misery come a few years sooner or later? If this youth deem himself happy now, yet let him sit with us for the sake of the wretchedness to come."

The poor idiot approached the young man with that mournful aspect of vacant inquiry which his face continually wore, and which caused people to say that he was always in search of his missing wits. After no little examination he touched the stranger's hand, but immediately drew back his own, shaking his head and shivering.

"Cold, cold, cold!" muttered the idiot.

The young man shivered too, and smiled.

"Gentlemen, and you, madam," said one of the stewards of the festival, "do not conceive so ill either of our caution or judgment, as to imagine that we have admitted this young stranger—Gervayse Hastings by name—without a full investigation and thoughtful balance of his claims. Trust me, not a guest at the table is better entitled to his seat."

The steward's guaranty was perforce satisfactory. The company, therefore, took their places, and addressed themselves to the serious business of the feast, but were soon disturbed by the hypochondriac, who thrust back his chair, complaining that a dish of stewed toads and vipers was set before him, and that there was green ditchwater in his cup of wine. This mistake being amended, he quietly resumed his seat. The wine, as it flowed freely from the sepulchral urn, seemed to come imbued with all gloomy inspirations; so that its influence was not to cheer, but either to sink the revellers into a deeper melancholy, or elevate their spirits to an enthusiasm of wretchedness. The conversation was various. They told sad stories about people who might have been Worthy guests at such a festival as the present. They talked of grisly incidents in human history; of strange crimes, which, if truly considered, were but convulsions of agony; of some lives that had been altogether wretched, and of others, which, wearing a general semblance of happiness, had yet been deformed, sooner or later, by misfortune, as by the intrusion of a grim face at a banquet; of death-bed scenes, and what dark intimations might be gathered from the words of dying men; of suicide, and whether the more eligible mode were by halter, knife, poison, drowning, gradual starvation, or the fumes of charcoal. The majority of the guests, as is the custom with people thoroughly and profoundly sick at heart, were anxious to make their own woes the theme of discussion, and prove themselves most excellent in anguish. The misanthropist went deep into the philosophy of evil, and wandered about in the darkness, with now and then a gleam of discolored light hovering on ghastly shapes and horrid scenery. Many a miserable thought, such as men have stumbled upon from age to age, did he now rake up again, and gloat over it as an inestimable gem, a diamond, a treasure far preferable to those bright, spiritual revelations of a better world, which are like precious stones from heaven's pavement. And then, amid his lore of wretchedness he hid his face and wept.

It was a festival at which the woful man of Uz might suitably have been a guest, together with all, in each succeeding age, who have tasted deepest of the bitterness of life. And be it said, too, that every son or daughter of woman, however favored with happy fortune, might, at one sad moment or another, have claimed the privilege of a stricken heart, to sit down at this table. But, throughout the feast, it was remarked that the young stranger, Gervayse Hastings, was unsuccessful in his attempts to catch its pervading spirit. At any deep, strong thought that found utterance, and which was torn out, as it were, from the saddest recesses of human consciousness, he looked mystified and bewildered; even more than the poor idiot, who seemed to grasp at such things with his earnest heart, and thus occasionally to comprehend them. The young man's conversation was of a colder and lighter kind, often brilliant, but lacking the powerful characteristics of a nature that had been developed by suffering.

"Sir," said the misanthropist, bluntly, in reply to some observation by Gervayse Hastings, "pray do not address me again. We have no right to talk together. Our minds have nothing in common. By what claim you appear at this banquet I cannot guess; but methinks, to a man who could say what you have just now said, my companions and myself must seem no more than shadows flickering on the wall. And precisely such a shadow are you to us."

The young man smiled and bowed, but, drawing himself back in his chair, he buttoned his coat over his breast, as if the banqueting-ball were growing chill. Again the idiot fixed his melancholy stare upon the youth, and murmured, "Cold! cold! cold!"

The banquet drew to its conclusion, and the guests departed. Scarcely had they stepped across the threshold of the hall, when the scene that had there passed seemed like the vision of a sick fancy, or an exhalation from a stagnant heart. Now and then, however, during the year that ensued, these melancholy people caught glimpses of one another, transient, indeed, but enough to prove that they walked the earth with the ordinary allotment of reality. Sometimes a pair of them came face to face, while stealing through the evening twilight, enveloped in their sable cloaks. Sometimes they casually met in churchyards. Once, also, it happened that two of the dismal banqueters mutually started at recognizing each other in the noonday sunshine of a crowded street, stalking there like ghosts astray. Doubtless they wondered why the skeleton did not come abroad at noonday too.

But whenever the necessity of their affairs compelled these Christmas guests into the bustling world, they were sure to encounter the young man who had so unaccountably been admitted to the festival. They saw him among the gay and fortunate; they caught the sunny sparkle of his eye; they heard the light and careless tones of his voice, and muttered to themselves with such indignation as only the aristocracy of wretchedness could kindle, "The traitor! The vile impostor! Providence, in its own good time, may give him a right to feast among us!" But the young man's unabashed eye dwelt upon their gloomy figures as they passed him, seeming to say, perchance with somewhat of a sneer, "First, know my secret then, measure your claims with mine!"

The step of Time stole onward, and soon brought merry Christmas round again, with glad and solemn worship in the churches, and sports, games, festivals, and everywhere the bright face of Joy beside the household fire. Again likewise the hall, with its curtains of dusky purple, was illuminated by the death-torches gleaming on the sepulchral decorations of the banquet. The veiled, skeleton sat in state, lifting the cypress-wreath above its head, as the guerdon of some guest illustrious in the qualifications which there claimed precedence. As the stewards deemed the world inexhaustible in misery, and were desirous of recognizing it in all its forms, they had not seen fit to reassemble the company of the former year. New faces now threw their gloom across the table.

There was a man of nice conscience, who bore a blood-stain in his heart—the death of a fellow-creature—which, for his more exquisite torture, had chanced with such a peculiarity of circumstances, that he could not absolutely determine whether his will had entered into the deed or not. Therefore, his whole life was spent in the agony of an inward trial for murder, with a continual sifting of the details of his terrible calamity, until his mind had no longer any thought, nor his soul any emotion, disconnected with it, There was a mother, too,—a mother once, but a desolation now,—who, many years before, had gone out on a pleasure-party, and, returning, found her infant smothered in its little bed. And ever since she has been tortured with the fantasy that her buried baby lay smothering in its coffin. Then there was an aged lady, who had lived from time immemorial with a constant tremor quivering through her-frame. It was terrible to discern her dark shadow tremulous upon the wall; her lips, likewise, were tremulous; and the expression of her eye seemed to indicate that her soul was trembling too. Owing to the bewilderment and confusion which made almost a chaos of her intellect, it was impossible to discover what dire misfortune had thus shaken her nature to its depths; so that the stewards had admitted her to the table, not from any acquaintance with her history, but on the safe testimony of her miserable aspect. Some surprise was expressed at the presence of a bluff, red-faced gentleman, a certain Mr. Smith, who had evidently the fat of many a rich feast within him, and the habitual twinkle of whose eye betrayed a disposition to break forth into uproarious laughter for little cause or none. It turned out, however, that, with the best possible flow of spirits, our poor friend was afflicted with a physical disease of the heart, which threatened instant death on the slightest cachinnatory indulgence, or even that titillation of the bodily frame produced by merry thoughts. In this dilemma he had sought admittance to the banquet, on the ostensible plea of his irksome and miserable state, but, in reality, with the hope of imbibing a life-preserving melancholy.

A married couple had been invited from a motive of bitter humor, it being well understood that they rendered each other unutterably miserable whenever they chanced to meet, and therefore must necessarily be fit associates at the festival. In contrast with these was another couple still unmarried, who had interchanged their hearts in early life, but had been divided by circumstances as impalpable as morning mist, and kept apart so long that their spirits now found it impossible to meet, Therefore, yearning for communion, yet shrinking from one another and choosing none beside, they felt themselves companionless in life, and looked upon eternity as a boundless desert. Next to the skeleton sat a mere son of earth,—a hunter of the Exchange,—a gatherer of shining dust,—a man whose life's record was in his ledger, and whose soul's prison-house the vaults of the bank where he kept his deposits. This person had been greatly perplexed at his invitation, deeming himself one of the most fortunate men in the city; but the stewards persisted in demanding his presence, assuring him that he had no conception how miserable he was.

And now appeared a figure which we must acknowledge as our acquaintance of the former festival. It was Gervayse Hastings, whose presence had then caused so much question and criticism, and who now took his place with the composure of one whose claims were satisfactory to himself and must needs be allowed by others. Yet his easy and unruffled face betrayed no sorrow.

The well-skilled beholders gazed a moment into his eyes and shook their heads, to miss the unuttered sympathy—the countersign never to be falsified—of those whose hearts are cavern-mouths through which they descend into a region of illimitable woe and recognize other wanderers there.

"Who is this youth?" asked the man with a bloodstain on his conscience. "Surely he has never gone down into the depths! I know all the aspects of those who have passed through the dark valley. By what right is he among us?"

"Ah, it is a sinful thing to come hither without a sorrow," murmured the aged lady, in accents that partook of the eternal tremor which pervaded her whole being "Depart, young man! Your soul has never been shaken, and, therefore, I tremble so much the more to look at you."

"His soul shaken! No; I'll answer for it," said bluff Mr. Smith, pressing his hand upon his heart and making himself as melancholy as he could, for fear of a fatal explosion of laughter. "I know the lad well; he has as fair prospects as any young man about town, and has no more right among us miserable creatures than the child unborn. He never was miserable and probably never will be!"

"Our honored guests," interposed the stewards, "pray have patience with us, and believe, at least, that our deep veneration for the sacredness of this solemnity would preclude any wilful violation of it. Receive this young man to your table. It may not be too much to say, that no guest here would exchange his own heart for the one that beats within that youthful bosom!"

"I'd call it a bargain, and gladly, too," muttered Mr. Smith, with a perplexing mixture of sadness and mirthful conceit. "A plague upon their nonsense! My own heart is the only really miserable one in the company; it will certainly be the death of me at last!"

Nevertheless, as on the former occasion, the judgment of the stewards being without appeal, the company sat down. The obnoxious guest made no more attempt to obtrude his conversation on those about him, but appeared to listen to the table-talk with peculiar assiduity, as if some inestimable secret, otherwise beyond his reach, might be conveyed in a casual word. And in truth, to those who could understand and value it, there was rich matter in the upgushings and outpourings of these initiated souls to whom sorrow had been a talisman, admitting them into spiritual depths which no other spell can open. Sometimes out of the midst of densest gloom there flashed a momentary radiance, pure as crystal, bright as the flame of stars, and shedding such a glow upon the mysteries of life, that the guests were ready to exclaim, "Surely the riddle is on the point of being solved!" At such illuminated intervals the saddest mourners felt it to be revealed that mortal griefs are but shadowy and external; no more than the sable robes voluminously shrouding a certain divine reality, and thus indicating what might otherwise be altogether invisible to mortal eye.

"Just now," remarked the trembling old woman, "I seemed to see beyond the outside. And then my everlasting tremor passed away!"

"Would that I could dwell always in these momentary gleams of light!" said the man of stricken conscience. "Then the blood-stain in my heart would be washed clean away."

This strain of conversation appeared so unintelligibly absurd to good Mr. Smith, that he burst into precisely the fit of laughter which his physicians had warned him against, as likely to prove instantaneously fatal. In effect, he fell back in his chair a corpse, with a broad grin upon his face, while his ghost, perchance, remained beside it bewildered at its unpremeditated exit. This catastrophe of course broke up the festival.

"How is this? You do not tremble!" observed the tremulous old woman to Gervayse Hastings, who was gazing at the dead man with singular intentness. "Is it not awful to see him so suddenly vanish out of the midst of life,—this man of flesh and blood, whose earthly nature was so warm and strong? There is a never-ending tremor in my soul, but it trembles afresh at, this! And you are calm!"

"Would that he could teach me somewhat!" said Gervayse Hastings, drawing a long breath. "Men pass before me like shadows on the wall; their actions, passions, feelings, are flickerings of the light, and then they vanish! Neither the corpse, nor yonder skeleton, nor this old woman's everlasting tremor, can give me what I seek."

And then the company departed.

We cannot linger to narrate, in such detail, more circumstances of these singular festivals, which, in accordance with the founder's will, continued to be kept with the regularity of an established institution. In process of time the stewards adopted the custom of inviting, from far and near, those individuals whose misfortunes were prominent above other men's, and whose mental and moral development might, therefore, be supposed to possess a corresponding interest. The exiled noble of the French Revolution, and the broken soldier of the Empire, were alike represented at the table. Fallen monarchs, wandering about the earth, have found places at that forlorn and miserable feast. The statesman, when his party flung him off, might, if he chose it, be once more a great man for the space of a single banquet. Aaron Burr's name appears on the record at a period when his ruin—the profoundest and most striking, with more of moral circumstance in it than that of almost any other man—was complete in his lonely age. Stephen Guard, when his wealth weighed upon him like a mountain, once sought admittance of his own accord. It is not probable, however, that these men had any lesson to teach in the lore of discontent and misery which might not equally well have been studied in the common walks of life. Illustrious unfortunates attract a wider sympathy, not because their griefs are more intense, but because, being set on lofty pedestals, they the better serve mankind as instances and bywords of calamity.

It concerns our present purpose to say that, at each successive festival, Gervayse Hastings showed his face, gradually changing from the smooth beauty of his youth to the thoughtful comeliness of manhood, and thence to the bald, impressive dignity of age. He was the only individual invariably present. Yet on every occasion there were murmurs, both from those who knew his character and position, and from them whose hearts shrank back as denying his companionship in their mystic fraternity.

"Who is this impassive man?" had been asked a hundred times. "Has he suffered? Has he sinned? There are no traces of either. Then wherefore is he here?"

"You must inquire of the stewards or of himself," was the constant reply. "We seem to know him well here in our city, and know nothing of him but what is creditable and fortunate. Yet hither he comes, year after year, to this gloomy banquet, and sits among the guests like a marble statue. Ask yonder skeleton, perhaps that may solve the riddle!"

It was in truth a wonder. The life of Gervayse Hastings was not merely a prosperous, but a brilliant one. Everything had gone well with him. He was wealthy, far beyond the expenditure that was required by habits of magnificence, a taste of rare purity and cultivation, a love of travel, a scholar's instinct to collect a splendid library, and, moreover, what seemed a magnificent liberality to the distressed. He had sought happiness, and not vainly, if a lovely and tender wife, and children of fair promise, could insure it. He had, besides, ascended above the limit which separates the obscure from the distinguished, and had won a stainless reputation in affairs of the widest public importance. Not that he was a popular character, or had within him the mysterious attributes which are essential to that species of success. To the public he was a cold abstraction, wholly destitute of those rich lines of personality, that living warmth, and the peculiar faculty of stamping his own heart's impression on a multitude of hearts, by which the people recognize their favorites. And it must be owned that, after his most intimate associates had done their best to know him thoroughly, and love him warmly, they were startled to find how little hold he had upon their affections. They approved, they admired, but still in those moments when the human spirit most craves reality, they shrank back from Gervayse Hastings, as powerless to give them what they sought. It was the feeling of distrustful regret with which we should draw back the hand after extending it, in an illusive twilight, to grasp the hand of a shadow upon the wall.

As the superficial fervency of youth decayed, this peculiar effect of Gervayse Hastings's character grew more perceptible. His children, when he extended his arms, came coldly to his knees, but never climbed them of their own accord. His wife wept secretly, and almost adjudged herself a criminal because she shivered in the chill of his bosom. He, too, occasionally appeared not unconscious of the chillness of his moral atmosphere, and willing, if it might be so, to warm himself at a kindly fire. But age stole onward and benumbed him snore and more. As the hoar-frost began to gather on him his wife went to her grave, and was doubtless warmer there; his children either died or were scattered to different homes of their own; and old Gervayse Hastings, unscathed by grief,—alone, but needing no companionship,—continued his steady walk through life, and still one very Christmas day attended at the dismal banquet. His privilege as a guest had become prescriptive now. Had he claimed the head of the table, even the skeleton would have been ejected from its seat.

Finally, at the merry Christmas-tide, when he had numbered fourscore years complete, this pale, highbrowed, marble-featured old man once more entered the long-frequented hall, with the same impassive aspect that had called forth so much dissatisfied remark at his first attendance. Time, except in matters merely external, had done nothing for him, either of good or evil. As he took his place he threw a calm, inquiring glance around the table, as if to ascertain whether any guest had yet appeared, after so many unsuccessful banquets, who might impart to him the mystery—the deep, warm secret—the life within the life—which, whether manifested in joy or sorrow, is what gives substance to a world of shadows.

"My friends," said Gervayse Hastings, assuming a position which his long conversance with the festival caused to appear natural, "you are welcome! I drink to you all in this cup of sepulchral wine."

The guests replied courteously, but still in a manner that proved them unable to receive the old man as a member of their sad fraternity. It may be well to give the reader an idea of the present company at the banquet.

One was formerly a clergyman, enthusiastic in his profession, and apparently of the genuine dynasty of those old Puritan divines whose faith in their calling, and stern exercise of it, had placed them among the mighty of the earth. But yielding to the speculative tendency of the age, he had gone astray from the firm foundation of an ancient faith, and wandered into a cloud-region, where everything was misty and deceptive, ever mocking him with a semblance of reality, but still dissolving when he flung himself upon it for support and rest. His instinct and early training demanded something steadfast; but, looking forward, he beheld vapors piled on vapors, and behind him an impassable gulf between the man of yesterday and to-day, on the borders of which he paced to and fro, sometimes wringing his hands in agony, and often making his own woe a theme of scornful merriment. This surely was a miserable man. Next, there was a theorist,—one of a numerous tribe, although he deemed himself unique since the creation,— a theorist, who had conceived a plan by which all the wretchedness of earth, moral and physical, might be done away, and the bliss of the millennium at once accomplished. But, the incredulity of mankind debarring him from action, he was smitten with as much grief as if the whole mass of woe which he was denied the opportunity to remedy were crowded into his own bosom. A plain old man in black attracted much of the company's notice, on the supposition that he was no other than Father Miller, who, it seemed, had given himself up to despair at the tedious delay of the final conflagration. Then there was a man distinguished for native pride and obstinacy, who, a little while before, had possessed immense wealth, and held the control of a vast moneyed interest which he had wielded in the same spirit as a despotic monarch would wield the power of his empire, carrying on a tremendous moral warfare, the roar and tremor of which was felt at every fireside in the land. At length came a crushing ruin,—a total overthrow of fortune, power, and character,—the effect of which on his imperious and, in many respects, noble and lofty nature might have entitled him to a place, not merely at our festival, but among the peers of Pandemonium.

There was a modern philanthropist, who had become so deeply sensible of the calamities of thousands and millions of his fellow-creatures, and of the impracticableness of any general measures for their relief, that he had no heart to do what little good lay immediately within his power, but contented himself with being miserable for sympathy. Near him sat a gentleman in a predicament hitherto unprecedented, but of which the present epoch probably affords numerous examples. Ever since he was of capacity to read a newspaper, this person had prided himself on his consistent adherence to one political party, but, in the confusion of these latter days, had got bewildered and knew not whereabouts his party was. This wretched condition, so morally desolate and disheartening to a man who has long accustomed himself to merge his individuality in the mass of a great body, can only be conceived by such as have experienced it. His next companion was a popular orator who had lost his voice, and—as it was pretty much all that he had to lose—had fallen into a state of hopeless melancholy. The table was likewise graced by two of the gentler sex,—one, a half-starved, consumptive seamstress, the representative of thousands just as wretched; the other, a woman of unemployed energy, who found herself in the world with nothing to achieve, nothing to enjoy, and nothing even to suffer. She had, therefore, driven herself to the verge of madness by dark breedings over the wrongs of her sex, and its exclusion from a proper field of action. The roll of guests being thus complete, a side-table had been set for three or four disappointed office-seekers, with hearts as sick as death, whom the stewards had admitted partly because their calamities really entitled them to entrance here, and partly that they were in especial need of a good dinner. There was likewise a homeless dog, with his tail between his legs, licking up the crumbs and gnawing the fragments of the feast,—such a melancholy cur as one sometimes sees about the streets without a master, and willing to follow the first that will accept his service.

In their own way, these were as wretched a set of people as ever had assembled at the festival. There they sat, with the veiled skeleton of the founder holding aloft the cypress-wreath, at one end of the table, and at the other, wrapped in furs, the withered figure of Gervayse Hastings, stately, calm, and cold, impressing the company with awe, yet so little interesting their sympathy that he might have vanished into thin air without their once exclaiming, "Whither is he gone?"

"Sir," said the philanthropist, addressing the old man, "you have been so long a guest at this annual festival, and have thus been conversant with so many varieties of human affliction, that, not improbably, you have thence derived some great and important lessons. How blessed were your lot could you reveal a secret by which all this mass of woe might be removed!"

"I know of but one misfortune," answered Gervayse Hastings, quietly, "and that is my own."

"Your own!" rejoined the philanthropist. "And looking back on your serene and prosperous life, how can you claim to be the sole unfortunate of the human race?"

"You will not understand it," replied Gervayse Hastings, feebly, and with a singular inefficiency of pronunciation, and sometimes putting one word for another. "None have understood it, not even those who experience the like. It is a chillness, a want of earnestness, a feeling as if what should be my heart were a thing of vapor, a haunting perception of unreality! Thus seeming to possess all that other men have, all that men aim at, I have really possessed nothing, neither joy nor griefs. All things, all persons,—as was truly said to me at this table long and long ago,—have been like shadows flickering on the wall. It was so with my wife and children, with those who seemed my friends: it is so with yourselves, whom I see now before one. Neither have I myself any real existence, but am a shadow like the rest."

"And how is it with your views of a future life?" inquired the speculative clergyman.

"Worse than with you," said the old man, in a hollow and feeble tone; "for I cannot conceive it earnestly enough to feel either hope or fear. Mine,—mine is the wretchedness! This cold heart,—this unreal life! Ah! it grows colder still."

It so chanced that at this juncture the decayed ligaments of the skeleton gave way, and the dry hones fell together in a heap, thus causing the dusty wreath of cypress to drop upon the table. The attention of the company being thus diverted for a single instant from Gervayse Hastings, they perceived, on turning again towards him, that the old man had undergone a change. His shadow had ceased to flicker on the wall.

"Well, Rosina, what is your criticism?" asked Roderick, as he rolled up the manuscript.

"Frankly, your success is by no means complete," replied she. "It is true, I have an idea of the character you endeavor to describe; but it is rather by dint of my own thought than your expression."

"That is unavoidable," observed the sculptor, "because the characteristics are all negative. If Gervayse Hastings could have imbibed one human grief at the gloomy banquet, the task of describing him would have been infinitely easier. Of such persons—and we do meet with these moral monsters now and then—it is difficult to conceive how they came to exist here, or what there is in them capable of existence hereafter. They seem to be on the outside of everything; and nothing wearies the soul more than an attempt to comprehend them within its grasp."

The Heavenly Christmas Tree

By

Fyodor Dostoyevsky

I am a novelist, and I suppose I have made up this story. I write "I suppose," though I know for a fact that I have made it up, but yet I keep fancying that it must have happened somewhere at some time, that it must have happened on Christmas Eve in some great town in a time of terrible frost.

I have a vision of a boy, a little boy, six years old or even younger. This boy woke up that morning in a cold damp cellar. He was dressed in a sort of little dressing-gown and was shivering with cold. There was a cloud of white steam from his breath, and sitting on a box in the corner, he blew the steam out of his mouth and amused himself in his dullness watching it float away. But he was terribly hungry. Several times that morning he went up to the plank bed where his sick mother was lying on a mattress as thin as a pancake, with some sort of bundle under her head for a pillow. How had she come here? She must have come with her boy from some other town and suddenly fallen ill. The landlady who let the "corners" had been taken two days before to the police station, the lodgers were out and about as the holiday was so near, and the only one left had been lying for the last twenty-four hours dead drunk, not having waited for Christmas. In another corner of the room a wretched old woman of eighty, who had once been a children's nurse but was now left to die friendless, was moaning and groaning with rheumatism, scolding and grumbling at the boy so that he was afraid to go near her corner. He had got a drink of water in the outer room, but could not find a crust anywhere, and had been on the point of waking his mother a dozen times. He felt frightened at last in the darkness: it had long[152] been dusk, but no light was kindled. Touching his mother's face, he was surprised that she did not move at all, and that she was as cold as the wall. "It is very cold here," he thought. He stood a little, unconsciously letting his hands rest on the dead woman's shoulders, then he breathed on his fingers to warm them, and then quietly fumbling for his cap on the bed, he went out of the cellar. He would have gone earlier, but was afraid of the big dog which had been howling all day at the neighbour's door at the top of the stairs. But the dog was not there now, and he went out into the street.

Mercy on us, what a town! He had never seen anything like it before. In the town from which he had come, it was always such black darkness at night. There was one lamp for the whole street, the little, low-pitched, wooden houses were closed up with shutters, there was no one to be seen in the street after dusk, all the people shut themselves up in their houses, and there was nothing but the howling of packs of dogs, hundreds and thousands of them barking and howling all night. But there it was so warm and he was given food, while here—oh, dear, if he only had something to eat! And what a noise and rattle here, what light and what people, horses and carriages, and what a frost! The frozen steam hung in clouds over the horses, over their warmly breathing mouths; their hoofs clanged against the stones through the powdery snow, and every one pushed so, and—oh, dear, how he longed for some morsel to eat, and how wretched he suddenly felt. A policeman walked by and turned away to avoid seeing the boy.

Here was another street—oh, what a wide one, here he would be run over for certain; how everyone was shouting, racing and driving along, and the light, the light! And what was this? A huge glass window, and through the window a tree reaching up to the ceiling; it was a fir tree, and on it were ever so many lights, gold papers and apples and little dolls and horses; and there were children clean and dressed[153] in their best running about the room, laughing and playing and eating and drinking something. And then a little girl began dancing with one of the boys, what a pretty little girl! And he could hear the music through the window. The boy looked and wondered and laughed, though his toes were aching with the cold and his fingers were red and stiff so that it hurt him to move them. And all at once the boy remembered how his toes and fingers hurt him, and began crying, and ran on; and again through another window-pane he saw another Christmas tree, and on a table cakes of all sorts—almond cakes, red cakes and yellow cakes, and three grand young ladies were sitting there, and they gave the cakes to any one who went up to them, and the door kept opening, lots of gentlemen and ladies went in from the street. The boy crept up, suddenly opened the door and went in. Oh, how they shouted at him and waved him back! One lady went up to him hurriedly and slipped a kopeck into his hand, and with her own hands opened the door into the street for him! How frightened he was. And the kopeck rolled away and clinked upon the steps; he could not bend his red fingers to hold it tight. The boy ran away and went on, where he did not know. He was ready to cry again but he was afraid, and ran on and on and blew his fingers. And he was miserable because he felt suddenly so lonely and terrified, and all at once, mercy on us! What was this again? People were standing in a crowd admiring. Behind a glass window there were three little dolls, dressed in red and green dresses, and exactly, exactly as though they were alive. One was a little old man sitting and playing a big violin, the two others were standing close by and playing little violins and nodding in time, and looking at one another, and their lips moved, they were speaking, actually speaking, only one couldn't hear through the glass. And at first the boy thought they were alive, and when he grasped that they were dolls he laughed. He had never seen such dolls before, and had no idea there were such[154] dolls! And he wanted to cry, but he felt amused, amused by the dolls. All at once he fancied that some one caught at his smock behind: a wicked big boy was standing beside him and suddenly hit him on the head, snatched off his cap and tripped him up. The boy fell down on the ground, at once there was a shout, he was numb with fright, he jumped up and ran away. He ran, and not knowing where he was going, ran in at the gate of some one's courtyard, and sat down behind a stack of wood: "They won't find me here, besides it's dark!"

He sat huddled up and was breathless from fright, and all at once, quite suddenly, he felt so happy: his hands and feet suddenly left off aching and grew so warm, as warm as though he were on a stove; then he shivered all over, then he gave a start, why, he must have been asleep. How nice to have a sleep here! "I'll sit here a little and go and look at the dolls again," said the boy, and smiled thinking of them. "Just as though they were alive!..." And suddenly he heard his mother singing over him. "Mammy, I am asleep; how nice it is to sleep here!"

"Come to my Christmas tree, little one," a soft voice suddenly whispered over his head.

He thought that this was still his mother, but no, it was not she. Who it was calling him, he could not see, but some one bent over and embraced him in the darkness; and he stretched out his hands to him, and ... and all at once—oh, what a bright light! Oh, what a Christmas tree! And yet it was not a fir tree, he had never seen a tree like that! Where was he now? Everything was bright and shining, and all round him were dolls; but no, they were not dolls, they were little boys and girls, only so bright and shining. They all came flying round him, they all kissed him, took him and carried him along with them, and he was flying himself, and he saw that his mother was looking at him and laughing joyfully. "Mammy, Mammy; oh, how nice it is here, Mammy!" And again he kissed the children and wanted to tell them at[155] once of those dolls in the shop window. "Who are you, boys? Who are you, girls?" he asked, laughing and admiring them.

"This is Christ's Christmas tree," they answered. "Christ always has a Christmas tree on this day, for the little children who have no tree of their own...." And he found out that all these little boys and girls were children just like himself; that some had been frozen in the baskets in which they had as babies been laid on the doorsteps of well-to-do Petersburg people, others had been boarded out with Finnish women by the Foundling and had been suffocated, others had died at their starved mother's breasts (in the Samara famine), others had died in the third-class railway carriages from the foul air; and yet they were all here, they were all like angels about Christ, and He was in the midst of them and held out His hands to them and blessed them and their sinful mothers.... And the mothers of these children stood on one side weeping; each one knew her boy or girl, and the children flew up to them and kissed them and wiped away their tears with their little hands, and begged them not to weep because they were so happy.

And down below in the morning the porter found the little dead body of the frozen child on the woodstack; they sought out his mother too.... She had died before him. They met before the Lord God in heaven.

Why have I made up such a story, so out of keeping with an ordinary diary, and a writer's above all? And I promised two stories dealing with real events! But that is just it, I keep fancying that all this may have happened really—that is, what took place in the cellar and on the woodstack; but as for Christ's Christmas tree, I cannot tell you whether that could have happened or not.

The Fir Tree

By

Hans Christian Andersen

Far away in the forest, where the warm sun and the fresh air made a sweet resting place, grew a pretty little fir tree. The situation was all that could be desired; and yet it was not happy, it wished so much to be like its tall companions, the pines and firs which grew around it.

The sun shone, and the soft air fluttered its leaves, and the little peasant children passed by, prattling merrily; but the fir tree did not heed them.

Sometimes the children would bring a large basket of raspberries or strawberries, wreathed in straws, and seat themselves near the fir tree, and say, "Is it not a pretty little tree?" which made it feel even more unhappy than before.

And yet all this while the tree grew a notch or joint taller every year; for by the number of joints in the stem of a fir tree we can discover its age.

Still, as it grew, it complained: "Oh! how I wish I were as tall as the other trees; then I would spread out my branches on every side, and my crown would overlook the wide world around. I should have the birds building their nests on my boughs, and when the wind blew, I should bow with stately dignity, like my tall companions."

So discontented was the tree, that it took no pleasure in the warm sunshine, the birds, or the rosy clouds that floated over it morning and evening.

Sometimes in winter, when the snow lay white and glittering on the ground, there was a little hare that would come springing along, and jump right over the little tree's head; then how mortified it would feel.

Two winters passed; and when the third arrived, the tree had grown so tall that the hare was obliged to run round it. Yet it remained unsatisfied, and would exclaim, "Oh! to grow, to grow; if I could but keep on growing tall and old! There is nothing else worth caring for in the world."

In the autumn the woodcutters came, as usual, and cut down several of the tallest trees; and the young fir, which was now grown to its full height, shuddered as the noble trees fell to the earth with a crash.

After the branches were lopped off, the trunks looked so slender and bare that they could scarcely be recognized. Then they were placed, one upon another, upon wagons, and drawn by horses out of the forest. "Where could they be going? What would become of them?" The young fir tree wished very much to know.

So in the spring, when the swallows and the storks came, it asked, "Do you know where those trees were taken? Did you meet them?"

The swallows knew nothing; but the stork, after a little reflection, nodded his head, and said, "Yes, I think I do. As I flew from Egypt, I saw several new ships, and they had fine masts that smelt like fir. These must have been the trees; and I assure you they were stately; they sailed right gloriously!"

"Oh, how I wish I were tall enough to go on the sea," said the fir tree. "Tell me what is this sea, and what does it look like?"

"It would take too much time to explain, a great deal too much," said the stork, flying quickly away.

"Rejoice in thy youth," said the sunbeam; "rejoice in thy fresh growth, and in the young life that is in thee."

And the wind kissed the tree, and the dew watered it with tears; but the fir tree regarded them not.

Christmas time drew near, and many young trees were cut down, some that were even smaller and younger than the fir tree, who enjoyed neither rest nor peace with longing to leave its forest home. These young trees, which were chosen for their beauty, kept their branches, and were also laid on wagons, and drawn by horses far away out of the forest.

"Where are they going?" asked the fir tree. "They are not taller than I am; indeed, one is not so tall. And why do they keep all their branches? Where are they going?"

"We know, we know," sang the sparrows; "we have looked in at the windows of the houses in the town, and we know what is done with them. Oh! you cannot think what honor and glory they receive. They are dressed up in the most splendid manner. We have seen them standing in the middle of a warm room, and adorned with all sorts of beautiful things;—honey cakes, gilded apples, playthings, and many hundreds of wax tapers."

"And then," asked the fir tree, trembling in all its branches, "and then what happens?"

"We did not see any more," said the sparrows; "but this was enough for us."

"I wonder whether anything so brilliant will ever happen to me," thought the fir tree. "It would be better even than crossing the sea. I long for it almost with pain. Oh, when will Christmas be here? I am now as tall and well grown as those which were taken away last year. Oh, that I were now laid on the wagon, or standing in the warm room, with all that brightness and splendor around me! Something better and more beautiful is to come after, or the trees would not be so decked out. Yes, what follows will be grander and more splendid. What can it be? I am weary with longing. I scarcely know what it is that I feel."

"Rejoice in our love," said the air and the sunlight. "Enjoy thine own bright life in the fresh air."

But the tree would not rejoice, though it grew taller every day and, winter and summer, its dark green foliage might be seen in the forests, while passersby would say, "What a beautiful tree!"

A short time before Christmas the discontented fir tree was the first to fall. As the axe cut sharply through the stem, and divided the pith, the tree fell with a groan to the earth, conscious of pain and faintness, and forgetting all its dreams of happiness, in sorrow at leaving its home in the forest. It knew that it should never again see its dear old companions, the trees, nor the little bushes and many-colored flowers that had grown by its side; perhaps not even the birds. Nor was the journey at all pleasant.

The tree first recovered itself while being unpacked in the courtyard of a house, with several other trees; and it heard a man say, "We only want one, and this is the prettiest. This is beautiful!"

Then came two servants in grand livery, and carried the fir tree into a large and beautiful apartment. Pictures hung on the walls, and near the great stove stood great china vases, with lions on the lids. There were rocking chairs, silken sofas, large tables covered with pictures, books, and playthings that had cost a hundred times a hundred dollars; at least so said the children.

Then the fir tree was placed in a large tub, full of sand; but green baize hung all around it, so that no one could know it was a tub; and it stood on a very handsome carpet. Oh, how the fir tree trembled! What was going to happen to him now? Some young ladies came in, and the servants helped them to adorn the tree.

On one branch they hung little bags cut out of colored paper, and each bag was filled with sweetmeats. From other branches hung gilded apples and walnuts, and all around were hundreds of red, blue and white tapers, which were fastened upon the branches. Dolls, exactly like real men and women, were placed under the green leaves,—and the tree had never seen such things before,—and at the top was fastened a glittering star, made of gold tinsel. Oh, it was very beautiful. "This evening," they all exclaimed, "how bright it will be!"

"Oh, that the evening were come," thought the tree, "and the tapers lighted! Then I should know what else is going to happen. Will the trees of the forest come to see me? Will the sparrows peep in at the windows, I wonder, as they fly? Shall I grow faster here, and keep on all these ornaments during summer and winter?" But guessing was of very little use. His back ached with trying; and this pain is as bad for a slender fir tree as headache is for us.

At last the tapers were lighted, and then what a glistening blaze of splendor the tree presented! It trembled so with joy in all its branches, that one of the candles fell among the green leaves and burnt some of them. "Help! help!" exclaimed the young ladies; but there was no danger, for they quickly extinguished the fire.

After this the tree tried not to tremble at all, though the fire frightened him, he was so anxious not to hurt any of the beautiful ornaments, even while their brilliancy dazzled him.

And now the folding doors were thrown open, and a troop of children rushed in as if they intended to upset the tree, and were followed more slowly by their elders. For a moment the little ones stood silent with astonishment, and then they shouted for joy till the room rang; and they danced merrily round the tree, while one present after another was taken from it.

"What are they doing? What will happen next?" thought the tree. At last the candles burned down to the branches, and were put out. Then the children received permission to plunder the tree.

Oh, how they rushed upon it! There was such a riot that the branches cracked, and had it not been fastened with the glistening star to the ceiling, it must have been thrown down.

Then the children danced about with their pretty toys, and no one noticed the tree, except the children's maid, who came and peeped among the branches to see if an apple or a fig had been forgotten.

"A story, a story," cried the children, pulling a little fat man toward the tree.

"Now we shall be in green shade," said the man, as he seated himself under it, "and the tree will have the pleasure of hearing also; but I shall only relate one story. What shall it be? Ivede-Avede, or Humpty-Dumpty, who fell down stairs, but soon got up again, and at last married a princess?"

"Ivede-Avede," cried some. "Humpty-Dumpty," cried others; and there was a famous uproar. But the fir tree remained quite still, and thought to himself, "Shall I have anything to do with all this? Ought I to make a noise too?" but he had already amused them as much as they wished.

Then the old man told them the story of Humpty-Dumpty;—how he fell downstairs and was raised up again, and married a princess. And the children clapped their hands and cried "Tell another, tell another," for they wanted to hear the story of Ivede-Avede; but this time they had only Humpty-Dumpty. After this the fir tree became quite silent and thoughtful. Never had the birds in the forest told such tales as Humpty-Dumpty who fell down stairs, and yet married a princess.

"Ah, yes! so it happens in the world," thought the fir tree. He believed it all, because it was related by such a pleasant man.

"Ah, well!" he thought, "who knows? Perhaps I may fall down too and marry a princess;" and he looked forward joyfully to the next evening, expecting to be again decked out with lights and playthings, gold and fruit. "Tomorrow I will not tremble," thought he; "I will enjoy all my splendor, and I shall hear the story of Humpty-Dumpty again, and perhaps Ivede-Avede." And the tree remained quiet and thoughtful all night.

In the morning the servants and the housemaid came in. "Now," thought the fir tree, "all my splendor is going to begin again." But they dragged him out of the room and upstairs to the garret and threw him on the floor, in a dark corner where no daylight shone, and there they left him. "What does this mean?" thought the tree. "What am I to do here? I can hear nothing in a place like this;" and he leaned against the wall and thought and thought.

And he had time enough to think, for days and nights passed, and no one came near him; and when at last somebody did come, it was only to push away some large boxes in a corner. So the tree was completely hidden from sight as if it had never existed.

"It is winter now," thought the tree; "the ground is hard and covered with snow, so that people cannot plant me. I shall be sheltered here, I dare say, until spring comes. How thoughtful and kind everybody is to me! Still, I wish this place were not so dark and so dreadfully lonely, with not even a little hare to look at. How pleasant it was out in the forest while the snow lay on the ground, when the hare would run by, yes, and jump over me too, although I did not like it then. Oh! it is terribly lonely here."

"Squeak, squeak," said a little mouse, creeping cautiously towards the tree; then came another, and they both sniffed at the fir tree, and crept in and out between the branches.

"Oh, it is very cold here," said the little mouse. "If it were not, we would be very comfortable here, wouldn't we, old fir tree?"

"I am not old," said the fir tree. "There are many who are older than I am."

"Where do you come from?" asked the mice, who were full of curiosity; "and what do you know? Have you seen the most beautiful places in the world, and can you tell us all about them? And have you been in the storeroom, where cheeses lie on the shelf and hams hang from the ceiling? One can run about on tallow candles there; one can go in thin and come out fat."

"I know nothing of that," said the fir tree; "but I know the wood where the sun shines and the birds sing." And then the tree told the little mice all about its youth. They had never heard such an account in their lives; and after they had listened to it attentively, they said, "What a number of things you have seen! You must have been very happy."

"Happy!" exclaimed the fir tree; and then, as he reflected on what he had been telling them, he said, "Ah, yes! after all, those were happy days." But when he went on and related all about Christmas eve, and how he had been dressed up with cakes and lights, the mice said, "How happy you must have been, you old fir tree."

"I am not old at all," replied the tree; "I only came from the forest this winter. I am now checked in my growth."

"What splendid stories you can tell," said the little mice. And the next night four other mice came with them to hear what the tree had to tell. The more he talked, the more he remembered, and then he thought to himself, "Yes, those were happy days; but they may come again. Humpty-Dumpty fell downstairs, and yet he married a princess. Perhaps I may marry a princess too." And the fir tree thought of the pretty little birch tree that grew in the forest; a real princess, a beautiful princess, she was to him.

"Who is Humpty-Dumpty?" asked the little mice. And then the tree related the whole story; he could remember every single word. And the little mice were so delighted with it, that they were ready to jump to the top of the tree. The next night a great many more mice made their appearance, and on Sunday two rats came with them; but they said it was not a pretty story at all, and the little mice were very sorry, for it made them also think less of it.

"Do you know only that one story?" asked the rats.

"Only that one," replied the fir tree. "I heard it on the happiest evening of my life; but I did not know I was so happy at the time."

"We think it is a very miserable story," said the rats. "Don't you know any story about bacon or tallow in the storeroom?"

"No," replied the tree.

"Many thanks to you, then," replied the rats, and they went their ways.

The little mice also kept away after this, and the tree sighed and said, "It was very pleasant when the merry little mice sat around me and listened while I talked. Now that is all past too. However, I shall consider myself happy when someone comes to take me out of this place."

But would this ever happen? Yes; one morning people came to clear up the garret; the boxes were packed away, and the tree was pulled out of the corner and thrown roughly on the floor; then the servants dragged it out upon the staircase where the daylight shone.

"Now life is beginning again," said the tree, rejoicing in the sunshine and fresh air. Then it was carried downstairs and taken into the courtyard so quickly that it forgot to think of itself, and could only look about, there was so much to be seen.

The court was close to a garden, where everything looked blooming. Fresh and fragrant roses hung over the little palings. The linden trees were in blossom; while the swallows flew here and there crying, "Twit, twit, twit, my mate is coming;" but it was not the fir tree they meant.

"Now I shall live," cried the tree joyfully, spreading out its branches; but alas! they were all withered and yellow, and it lay in a corner amongst weeds and nettles. The star of gold paper still stuck in the top of the tree, and glittered in the sunshine.

In the same courtyard two of the merry children were playing who had danced round the tree at Christmas time and had been so happy. The youngest saw the gilded star and ran and pulled it off the tree. "Look what is sticking to the ugly old fir tree," said the child, treading on the branches till they crackled under his boots.

And the tree saw all the fresh, bright flowers in the garden, and then looked at itself, and wished it had remained in the dark corner of the garret. It thought of its fresh youth in the forest, of the merry Christmas evening, and of the little mice who had listened to the story of Humpty-Dumpty.

"Past! past!" said the poor tree. "Oh, had I but enjoyed myself while I could have done so! but now it is too late."

Then a lad came and chopped the tree into small pieces, till a large bundle lay in a heap on the ground. The pieces were placed in the fire, and they blazed up brightly, while the tree sighed so deeply that each sigh was like a little pistol shot. Then the children, who were at play, came and seated themselves in front of the fire and looked at it, and cried, "Pop, pop." But at each "pop," which was a deep sigh, the tree was thinking of a summer day in the forest, or of some winter night there when the stars shone brightly, and of Christmas evening and of Humpty-Dumpty, the only story it had ever heard, or knew how to relate,—till at last it was consumed.

The boys still played in the garden, and the youngest wore the golden star on his breast with which the tree had been adorned during the happiest evening of its existence. Now all was past; the tree's life was past, and the story also past! for all stories must come to an end some time or other.

Little Paulina

A Story of Russian Life

By

Anna Robinson

One day, in Russia, there was a heavy snowstorm. The snow was deep on the ground; and in the forest the branches of the trees bent under its weight.

In this forest a little girl was struggling along. There was no path for her to follow, for the snow covered all the paths. The little girl's name was Paulina. She was dressed in a long fur coat, and she wore a cap and mittens and gaiters of fur, so that she looked more like a little furry animal than a little girl. She kept tramping along, not a bit afraid, when suddenly she heard a call for help.

"Help! Help!" the call came.

"Coming, coming!" she called back. She went in the direction of the voice and soon she saw a man making his way toward her. His dress was that of a peasant.

"Will you please direct me out of this forest, little one?" he asked. "You probably know the paths about."

"No, I am a stranger here," Paulina answered. "I live in Kief—that is, I did live there; but I am on my way to my father."

"Where is your father?" asked the man.

"He is in Siberia. They banished him."

"But, little one," said the stranger, "that is a terrible place for a child to go to. That frozen country, where wicked people are sent!"

"O, yes,—but my father is there, you know," said Paulina.

"Who is your father?" the man asked.

The little girl was about to tell him, when she noticed a look of interest on the stranger's face, so she said,

"Did you say that you had lost your way in the forest? Do you live far from here?"

"Yes, very far. I am lost, and am nearly perishing from hunger and cold. How far is it to the next village?"

"They told me it was some miles on," said the child. "But I will take you back to the woodsman's cottage where I spent the night. The woman is a kind-hearted person, and I am sure she will give you shelter."

"That is kind of you, little one," said the stranger, "but you will be hindering your own journey if you do that."

"I know that my father would want me to show a kindness, even though it did put me back some," Paulina said.

"You must have a good father, to give you such training. Why did the Emperor send him into exile?" the stranger asked her.

"O, my father had enemies who lied to the Emperor—and there was no chance given to my father to explain. So the Emperor sent him away to Siberia,—and I am trying to find my way there to him."

While they walked through the forest, the stranger told Paulina about his own little daughter who was expecting him to spend Christmas with her. At last they reached the woodsman's hut. The woman greeted them kindly, and while Paulina went into another room to help her prepare the evening meal, the stranger was left warming himself by the fire, and rocking the cradle.

Once Paulina thought she heard voices, as if the stranger were talking to someone; but when she went back, she found him alone, still warming his hands and rocking the cradle with his foot.

That night the stranger slept on the floor in front of the fire—there was no other place for him; but he was glad to be safe from the storm outside.

Early in the morning, the two started out through the forest again. They must hurry, if they were to reach the next village before darkness fell. The storm had passed over, and the day was cold and clear. A beautiful winter's day. The little girl and the stranger reached the village on the other side of the forest early in the afternoon, and there before them they saw a beautiful sleigh drawn by four horses. There were four servants standing near.

"What a lovely sleigh!" exclaimed Paulina.

"Yes, I wonder where they are going. I will ask them," the stranger said. He went nearer the men and spoke to them.

"We are driving for our master to Igorhof," they said.

"Why, that is where my daughter is. If I might only ride with you, I could spend Christmas with her. Tomorrow is Christmas day, you know. And, little one, you could spend Christmas with us, too."

"O, no," said Paulina. "I could not take the time. I must hurry on to my father. But it would be lovely if we could only ride in this beautiful sleigh."

"You could spend the night with us, and then we could set you on your way, because you have been so kind to me," the man told her.

The servants were willing to let them ride in the beautiful sleigh, and soon they were speeding over the snow toward the great city. Once, the stranger took a scarf from a pocket on the side of the sleigh and threw it about his neck. Paulina frowned, and promptly placed it back in the pocket.

"It isn't right for you to touch anything in the sleigh. It belongs to someone else. I am beginning to fear that you may not be an honest man," she said gravely.

The stranger laughed at her, but he did not take the scarf again. They sped on over the snow until, as darkness fell, they reached the city. Soon they entered a large courtyard, and the stranger took Paulina's hand and led her into a narrow passageway, and up a small winding stairway.

"Where are you taking me?" asked Paulina. "I feel almost sure now, that you are not an honest man. I think that you may even be a thief!"

The man laughed again.

"No, I am an honest man. You will believe me when you see my little daughter. I trusted you in the forest. Now you trust me."

He led her into a large room, and they sat down upon a sofa.

"We will wait here until my daughter comes," he said.

Soon the door opened, and a beautiful little girl, about as large as Paulina, came toward them. She looked puzzled when she saw the rough-looking man with the little girl. She went close to the stranger and looked into his face.

"It *is* my father!" she cried, and threw her arms around his neck.

"But why are you dressed like a peasant? Has there been an accident? And who is this little stranger?"

The man took her on his lap and told her how his sleigh had been overturned in the storm, and how he had found his way to a peasant's hut, where they had given him dry clothes to put on, and how he had started out alone to find his way through the forest; and how he was nearly perishing with cold and hunger when this little girl had rescued him, and how, if it had not been for her, he would have died in the snow in the forest. He told her how little Paulina was on her way to Siberia to find her father, and how they went to the woodsman's hut where a servant had found him, and how he had planned for the sleigh to meet them on the other side of the forest.

"O," Paulina interrupted him, "then there was somebody talking with you when we were preparing the evening meal?"

"Yes, and everything came out just as I had planned. And do you know, little daughter, this Paulina would not let me put my own scarf around my neck. She thought that I was a thief. She is an honest little girl. But she will not tell me her name. She does not trust me."

"But why should I trust you, when you will not tell me who you are, or anything about yourself?" Paulina asked.

"Do trust my father, Paulina. I'm sure he can help you. He will tell you who he is soon, I know," the beautiful little girl said.

"Yes, little one," the stranger said. "I know someone who could speak to the Emperor about your father, and perhaps he could be pardoned. Please tell me your name; and then before you go away I will answer any questions about myself you may ask me."

"Do tell my father, Paulina," the little girl urged.

Paulina threw her arms about the stranger's knees.

"O, if you could only get the Emperor to pardon him.— But I do not ask for a *pardon*—he has done nothing to be pardoned for. All that I ask is that he may have justice done him. My father is Vladimir Betzkoi."

The stranger frowned, and then he whispered,

"There must be some mistake. He must be a good man to have such an honest little daughter." Then he said to Paulina,

"Do you believe now that I am an honest man, since you have seen my daughter?"

"O, yes, indeed I do. You couldn't help being good and honest. She is so beautiful. I think her face is like what a queen's should be," Paulina answered eagerly.

The stranger and his little daughter smiled, and the man said,

"Well, I believe that your father is an honest man since I have seen you. And I can tell you now, I *know* he will be pardoned."

"Tell her, father, tell the little Paulina who you are," his daughter whispered.

"Until your father returns to you, little one, you must stay here and I will be a father to you—as I am father to all the people of Russia, for *I am the Emperor!*"

Just then the bells began ringing, and voices outside began singing,—for it was the beginning of Christmas morning. And Paulina said,

"This is the happiest Christmas morning I have ever known."

The Shepherd's Story

By

Washington Gladden

"Bring hither that sheepskin, Joseph, and lay it down on this bank of dry earth, under this shelving rock. The wind blows chilly from the west, but the rock will shelter us. The sky is fair and the moon is rising, and we can sit here and watch the flocks on the hillside below. Your young blood and your father's coat of skins will keep you warm for one watch, I am sure. At midnight, my son, your father, Reuben, and his brother James will take our places; for the first watch the old man and the boy will tend the sheep."

"Yes, grandfather; you shall sit in that snug corner of the rock, where you can lean back and take your comfort. I will lie here at your feet. Now and then I will run to see whether the sheep are wandering, and that will warm me, if I grow cold."

"Have you never been out on the hills at night with your father?"

"Never, grandfather. I have often begged him to let me come; but he kept saying that I must wait until I was twelve years old. On the last full moon was my birthday and today, when he returned from Bethlehem to the flocks, he brought me with him."

"So this is the lad's first night with the sheep in the fields, and the old man's last night, I fear," said the aged shepherd, sadly. "It is not often in these days that I venture out to keep the watches of the flock; but this one night of the year I have spent upon these hills these many years, and I always shall as long as I have strength to walk so far."

"Was your father, too, a shepherd?"

"Yes, and all his fathers before him for many generations. On these hills my ancestors have kept their sheep for I know not how long."

Joseph was still for a moment. His eyes wandered away over the silent hills, lit by the rising moon. His face was troubled. At length, he said gently:

"Grandfather, I heard Rabbi Eliezer saying, the other day, in the synagogue, that a shepherd's life is not a noble life. He was reading from one of the old doctors, who said: 'Let no one make his son a camel-driver, a barber, a sailor, a shepherd, or a shopkeeper. They are dishonest callings.' I was angry when he read it; but I held my peace."

"You did well, my son, to hold your peace. I myself have often heard such words, of late, from the doctors in the synagogues; but it is not wise to answer them. Where they got their notions, I know not. From the Egyptians, I think, more than from the prophets. All Egyptians hate shepherds, and can never speak of them without sneering. Perhaps they have not yet forgotten how the shepherds conquered and ruled them for generations. Nevertheless, there is some reason why the calling of the shepherds should be despised. Many of them are rude and fierce men. Living out of doors so constantly makes their manners rough and their temper harsh. They are often quarrelsome. Such bloody fights as I used to see among them, at the wells in the south country, where they brought their flocks to water and each one wanted the first chance at the well, I hope you will never look upon."

"But all shepherds are not so," protested Joseph.

"No, indeed. Brave men they must be; fleet of foot and strong of limb and stout of heart; but brave men are not always quarrelsome. Many a shepherd whom I have known had a heart as pure and gentle as a child's. And the godliest men that I have known have been among them. If the shepherd has but learned to think, to commune with his own soul, he has time for thought and time for prayer. More than one with whom I have watched upon these hills knew all the Psalms of David by heart and many of the books of the prophets. The doctors in the synagogues teach only the law; the shepherds love best the Psalms and the prophets. They do not forget that King David was himself a shepherd's lad. It was upon these very hills that he kept his father's sheep. It was in that ravine over yonder, on that hillside, that he, a mere stripling, caught by the beard and killed the lion and the bear that attacked the sheep. It was on that slope, just a little to the south, that the messenger found him with his flocks when he was called home to be anointed by Samuel the prophet. When the doctors talk so contemptuously about the shepherds, I wonder if they do not remember that the great king wrote: 'The Lord is my Shepherd.' How can our calling be so mean as they say, when David, who was called from the sheepfolds, praises the Eternal One himself as his Shepherd? But hark! what noise is that I hear? There is some trouble among the sheep."

"Let me run and see," answers the boy, "and I will come and bring you word."

So saying, Joseph cast off his father's shaggy coat, seized the sling in his left hand and the crook in his right and ran swiftly out to the brow of the hill. He was a strong lad, large of frame and a swift runner, and the sling in his hand was a sure weapon. The old man looked after him with pride, as he bounded over the rocks, and said to himself:

"Some evil beast, I doubt not. But the lad's heart is brave and he must learn to face dangers. I will wait a moment."

Presently the sheep came huddling round the hill in terror. The quick, faint bleat of the ewes showed that they had seen a foe. The old man arose and hurried in the direction in which the lad had disappeared. Joseph was just returning, breathless, from the ravine below.

"It was a wolf, grandfather. The sheep on this side of the ledge had seen him and were flying. Just as I reached the brow of the hill, he was creeping round the end of the ledge below, ready to spring upon a ewe that was feeding near. The first thing he knew a stone from my sling hit him, and he went howling down the hill. I think I broke his leg, for he went on three legs and I gained on him as I ran after him; but he crawled into a narrow place among the rocks in the gorge down yonder, and I could not follow him."

"Well done, my lad," said the ancient Stephanus proudly. "You will make a good shepherd. These single wolves are cowards. It is always safe to face them. When they come in packs, it is quite another thing. But this fellow will keep at a safe distance for the rest of the night, you may depend. Let us go back to our shelter and call the sheep together."

It was several minutes before Stephanus and Joseph could collect the sheep that the wolf had scattered; but at length, with the aid of the dog, who was not a very brave specimen, and who had taken to his heels when he saw the wolf coming, they succeeded in driving them into a safe neighborhood, and then, with their blood quickened by the adventure, they sat down again beneath the overhanging rock.

"You said, grandfather, that you always spent this night with the flocks in the fields. Why this night?" asked the boy.

"Do you not know, my boy, that this is the night of the year on which the Lord Christ was born?"

"Oh! yes," answered the lad. "My father told me as we were walking hither today, but I had forgotten it. And you were with the sheep that night?"

"Aye."

"Where was it?"

"Here, on this very spot."

The boy's eyes began to grow and fill with wonder and there was a slight tremor in his voice as he hurriedly plied the aged man with his eager questions. Stephanus drew his shepherd's cloak around him, and leaned forward a little, and looked out upon the silent moonlit hills, and then up into the sky.

"How long ago was that, grandfather?"

"Just fifty years ago this night."

"And how old were you then?"

"Fourteen, and a stout boy for my age. I had been for two years in the fields with my father, and had tasted to the full the hardships and dangers of the shepherd's life."

"Who were with you on that night?"

"My father, and his brother, James, and Hosea, the son of John, a neighbor and kinsman of ours. On that year, as on this year and often, there came in the midwinter a dry and warm season between the early and the latter rain. We had driven forth our flocks from Bethlehem and were dwelling by night in the shelter of the tower on the hillside yonder, watching and sleeping two and two. My father and I were wont to keep the early watches. At midnight we would call James and Hosea, and they would watch till the morning. But that night, when the sun went down and the stars came out, we were sitting here, upon this hillside, talking of the troubles of Israel and of the promises of deliverance spoken by the prophets; and James and Hosea were asking my father questions, and he was answering them, for he was older than they, and all the people of Bethlehem reverenced him as a wise and devout man. Some even said that, if the people of Israel had not ceased to look for prophets, they would have counted him a prophet. I remember well that, when he rose in the synagogue, it seemed as if some wisdom from on high touched his lips, and he would speak with such hope and courage of the light that should yet shine in our darkness and of the help that should yet arise to Judah, that the people's faces would glow with joyful expectation."

Stephanus paused a moment and started forward, as his eye was turned toward his own shadow upon the rock, cast by the rising moon. Did the old man's figure that he saw remind him of the patriarch of whom he was talking?

Soon he went on.

"Ah! but they should have heard my father talking here by night, under the stars. It was here upon these hills where the royal shepherd used to sing, that his tongue was loosed and he spoke wonderful words. So it was that night, fifty years ago. I remember it as if it were yesterday. My father sat in this very niche, where I am sitting now; James and Hosea were on either side of him. I was lying at their feet, as you now lie at mine. Their faces kindled and the tremor of deep feeling was in their voices as they talked together; and the other two had lingered here three or four hours after the sun had set. It was not a moonlit night like this, but all the stars were out and all the winds were still.

"Suddenly I saw my father rise to his feet. Then the other men sprang up, with astonishment and wonder upon their faces. It had grown light all at once, lighter than the brightest moon; and as I turned my face in the direction in which the others were looking, I saw, standing there upon that level place, a figure majestic and beautiful beyond all the power of words to tell."

"Were you not afraid, grandfather?"

"Indeed, I was, my boy. My heart stopped beating. The others were standing, but I had no power to rise. I lay there motionless upon the earth. My eyes were fixed upon that wonderful face; upon those clear, shining eyes; upon that brow that seemed to beam with the purity of the soul within. It was not a smile with which that face was lighted. It was something too noble and exalted to call by that name. It was a look that told of power and peace, of joy and triumph."

"Did you know that it was an angel?"

"I knew not anything. I only knew that what I saw was glorious, too glorious for mortal eyes to look upon. Yet, while I gazed, and in far less time than I have now taken to tell you of what I saw, the terribleness of the look began to disappear, the sweetness and grace of the soul shone forth, and I had almost ceased to tremble before the angel opened his mouth. And when he spoke, his voice, clearer than any trumpet and sweeter than any lute, charmed away all my fears."

"'Be not afraid' he said, 'for behold I bring you good tidings of great joy which shall be to all people. For there is born to you this day, in the City of David, a Savior, which is Messiah, the King. And this is the sign unto you. Ye shall find a babe wrapped in swaddling clothes and lying in a manger.'

"Oh! that voice, my boy! It makes my heart beat now to remember its sweetness. It seemed to carry these words into our innermost hearts; to print them on our memory, so that we never could forget one syllable of what he said. And then, before we had time to make reply, he turned aside a little and lifted his face toward heaven, and, in a tone far louder than that in which he had spoken to us, but yet so sweet that it did not startle us at all, came forth from his lips the first strain of the great song:

"'Glory to God in the highest!'

"When he had uttered that, he paused a moment, and the echoes, one after another, from hills that were near and hills that were far away, came flying home to us; so that I knew for once what the prophet meant when he said that all the mountains and the hills should break forth into singing. But before the echoes had all faded we began to hear other voices above our heads, a great chorus, taking up the strain that the angel first had sung. At first it seemed dim and far away; but gradually it came nearer, and filled all the air, filled all the earth, filled all our souls with a most entrancing sweetness. Glory to God in the highest!—that was the grandest part. It seemed as though there could be no place so high that that strain would not mount up to it, and no place so happy that that voice would not make it thrill with new gladness. But then came the softer tones, less grand, but even sweeter: 'Peace on earth; good will to men.'

"Oh! my boy, if you had heard that music as I did, you would not wonder when I tell you that it has been hard for me to wait here, in the midst of the dreary noises of earth, for fifty years before hearing it again. But earth that night was musical as heaven. You should have heard the echoes that came back, when the angels' chorus ceased, from all these mountains and all these little hills on every side. There is music enough even in this world, if one can only call it forth; chords divine that will vibrate with wonderful harmony. It only needs an angel's hand to touch the trembling strings."

"Did you see the choir of angels overhead, grandfather?"

"Nay, I saw nothing. The brightness was too dazzling for mortal eyes. We all stood there, with downcast eyes, listening spell-bound to the wonderful melody, until the chorus ceased, and the echoes, one after another, died away, and the glory faded out of the sky and the stars came back again, and no sound was heard but the faint voice of a young lamb, calling for its mother.

"The first to break the silence was my father. 'Come,' he said, in a solemn voice. 'Let us go at once to Bethlehem, and see this thing which is come to pass, which the Lord hath made known unto us.'

"So the sheep were quietly gathered into the fold at the tower, and we hastened to Bethlehem. Never shall I forget that journey by night. We spake not many words, as we traveled swiftly the twenty furlongs; talk seemed altogether tame; but now and then my father broke forth in a song, and the others joined in the chorus. We were not so spent with running but that we could find voice for singing; and such words as these of the prophet were the only ones that could give voice to our swelling hearts:

"'Sing, O heavens; and be joyful, O earth; And break forth into singing, O mountains; For the Lord hath comforted His people, And will have mercy on His afflicted.

"'How beautiful upon the mountains Are the feet of Him that bringeth good tidings, That publisheth peace, That bringeth good tidings of good, That publisheth salvation.'

"It was midnight when we climbed the hill to the little city of Bethlehem; the constellation Cesil, called by the Greeks Orion, was just setting in the west. We knew not whither to go. We had only the sign of the angel by which we should know the infant Messiah. He was a babe of one day. He was lying in a manger.

"'Let us go to the inn Chimham,' said my father. 'It stands on the very spot where King David was born. Peradvanture we shall find him there.'

"Over the entrance to the court of the inn a lantern was swinging from a rope stretched across from post to post. Guided by its light, we entered, and found the courtyard full of beasts of burden, showing that the inn was crowded with travelers. In the arched shelter of the hostelry as many as could find room were lying; some who could not sleep were sitting up and waiting drearily for the morning. Two aged women near the entrance, were talking in a low tone.

"'Peace be unto you!' said my father.

"'The Lord be gracious unto thee,' answered the oldest woman, in a solemn voice, as she looked upon my father's white beard; 'but,' she quickly added, 'there is scanty cheer in this place for late comers.'

"'We seek not lodging,' said my father; 'but know you whether among these guests is an infant born this day?'

"'Verily there is,' answered the aged dame; 'a man-child more beautiful than any my eyes have ever beheld. He is lying in a manger there in the cave that serves for stable.'

"We hastened to the mouth of the cave, and there beheld our King. The oxen and the asses were lying near, and a strong man, with a grave and benignant face, was leaning on his staff above the manger. A beautiful young mother lay close beside it, her cheek resting on her hands, that were clasped over the edge of the rock-hewn crib. Into this a little straw had been thrown, and over it a purple robe had been cast, whereon the infant lay. A lamp, set upon a projection of the wall of the cave, burned brightly near. The great eyes of the wonderful child were wandering about the room; his hand touched his mother's lips. I waited to hear him open his mouth and speak.

"There was a moment of silence after we entered the cave. My father broke it with his salutation:

"'Hail, thou blessed among women!' he cried. 'This child of thine is a Prince and a Savior.'

"And then we all bowed low upon our faces before him and worshipped him with praise and gladness.

"The two aged women, with whom we had spoken, had followed us to the door of the stable, and, seeing us worshipping there, had run to call others who were awake in the inn, so that when we arose quite a company were standing at the door, or just within, gazing upon the King in his beauty and listening to our thanksgiving with great wonder.

"Then my father told them all the things that we had heard and seen—the message of the angel, the song in the air, the glory of the Lord that had appeared to us—and how we had quickly come to Bethlehem, and had found things as the angel had told us. 'And it is even,' he cried, 'as the prophet himself hath spoken: "Thou Bethlehem Ephratah, though thou be little among the thousands of Judah, yet out of thee shall he come forth unto me that is to be ruler in Israel, whose going forth hast been of old; even from everlasting."'

"All that heard were full of astonishment—all save the mother. I saw no wonder on her face; the great things that my father told caused her no astonishment; she listened with a quiet and solemn joy, like one who was saying in her heart: 'I knew it all before.'

"When my father had finished speaking, we all bowed low again before the young child; and the mother lifted him in her arms and placed his cheek against her own, smiling graciously on us, but uttering no word. And we came forth from the stable and stood again beneath the stars in the courtyard of the inn. By this time many of the travelers were awake, and an eager company had gathered around us, all of whom desired to be told of the sign that had been shown to us. To one and another we rehearsed our story, lingering long to make known the good tidings, until the morning star appeared and the dawn began to kindle over the eastern hills. Then we hastened to our own homes in the city, and told our kindred what had happened unto us. In the early morning we came back again unto our pastures and our flocks, rejoicing to stand again in the place where the glory of God had shone and the music of heaven had filled the air."

Stephanus paused, his face all aglow with the tale that he had been telling. His eyes swept again the circuit of the moonlit hills and were lifted reverently up to the sky.

"Did you ever see the Lord Christ after that?" asked Joseph.

"Once only. My father and I were at Jerusalem at the passover. It was the year before my father died, seventeen years ago; it was the same week on which our Lord was crucified. My father was then an aged man—fourscore and five years old. Our tent was pitched on the slope of the Mount of Olives, near the Bethany road. While we sat there one morning, a great noise of shouting was heard, and presently we saw one riding on an ass, followed by a great company, crying 'Hosanna!' As we drew nearer, we heard them say that it was Jesus of Nazareth; and, when we saw His face, we knew that it was He, by the wonderful eyes, though it was the face of a bearded man, and not of an infant, and was very pale and sad. As He drew near to our tent, the city came full into His view, with its gilded roofs and marble pinnacles, blazing under the morning sun. Suddenly He paused in the way, and we heard Him weeping aloud, though we could not hear His words of lamentation. The multitude halted, too, when we did; and the cheering ceased, and some of those who stood nearest Him wept also, though no one seemed to know what had caused His grief. But soon they went on again, and before they reached the foot of the hill another multitude met them, coming forth from the city, and we heard their shouts of 'Hosanna in the Highest!' as they entered the gate of Jerusalem."

"What said your father when he saw all this?" queried Joseph.

"He said but little. There was a shadow on his face, yet he spoke cheerfully. 'I cannot understand it,' he murmured. 'They are trying to make Him King of the

Jews; but King He will not be, at least not in their fashion. Yet in some way I know He will be Prince and Deliverer. I cannot understand, I will wait.'"

"Were you not in Jerusalem when He was put to death?"

"No. My father was frail and ill and we had hastened home to Bethlehem. News of His death on the cross had only just reached us when another messenger came to tell us that the sepulcher in which He had been laid was empty; that He had risen from the dead.

"My father's eyes kindled when he heard this message. He cast aside his staff and stood firm on his feet. His voice, when he spoke, rang out like a trumpet. 'Blessed be the Lord God of Israel!' he cried. It is thus that He redeemeth His people. This Jesus is not to be the Captain of our armies, but the Savior of our souls. His kingdom is the kingdom of righteousness, and therefore it is that the prophet hath said: "Of the increase of His government and peace there shall be no end."

"Always after that, words of the prophet concerning the Messiah kept coming back to my father; and once and again he cried out: 'Truly, this Jesus was the Son of God, the true King of Israel!' As the months wore on, his words were more and more of the crucified and risen Lord, and he dwelt in a great peace. At length, when the flocks were led forth to the midwinter pasturage, he begged to go with me. It was on this very day that we came, the same day of the year on which the Lord was born. He was feeble and tottered as he walked; but he leaned on my arm and we came slowly. In the evening he said: 'Let me go, my son, and sit once more under the great rock.' I wrapped him in my coat of skins, and sat here where I sit now and where he was sitting when the angel came. We talked here long, under the stars, that night, of Him whom we had learned to love as Master and Lord, of the works that He had done and the words that He had spoken, as His disciples had told of them. We had been silent for a few moments, when I looked up, and saw that his head had fallen backward against the rock wall. I sprang to him. His eyes were shut, but his lips were moving. I put my ear to his mouth, and heard him say only: 'Peace—on—earth—good will'— they were his last words. He had gone beyond our starlight, into the country where the light always shines—the glory that fell that night, fifty years ago, upon these hills of Bethlehem."

Stephanus was silent and Joseph's eyes were full of tears. At length the old man rose.

"Come, my son," he said. "Cesil is in the south; it is midnight; let us call your father and his brother. The old man and the boy have kept their watch, and it is now time for rest."

Printed in Great Britain
by Amazon

14440853R00144